Want a free Ebook? Join my mailing list to get my monthly newsletter!

UNSUITABLE

Hopeless Romantics

MATILDA MARTEL

UNSUITABLE

SUMMARY

Darla Jones knows all about keeping up with the Joneses. Those are her folks, the Prince and Princess of Park Avenue. Her grandfather was the King.

It's her birthright to live a life of luxury and hobnob with Manhattan's social elite, but this diminutive gal has dreams that don't involve following in her mother and sister's socialite footsteps.

She wants to make her own way. Somehow. If she can find something that clicks.

When she inherits her great-aunt's Brooklyn brownstone, she takes her chance to see a different side of life, sending her parents into a panic that she'll find an unsuitable match and live an unsuitable life.

Oscar Brennan's an unsuitable man.

He attended school with Darla's brother but happily gave up his scholarship to return home and help his ailing mother. He's never met his father. Unlike his good friend, Denver Jones, he became a lawyer to help people, not join fancy firms or run for office. He wants nothing to do with Manhattan. He's happy in

Brooklyn where people don't pretend to be something they're not.

Until Denver's baby sister moves next door. There's something about those big blue eyes, giant heart and well-intentioned cluelessness that turns his head. There's something about those kissable lips and sharp curves that make him come back for more.

He shouldn't look. He damn well shouldn't stare. She's Denver's sister. But offering his assistance feels like the right thing to do.

When she needs a date to her sister's wedding, he happily obliges to keep her from taking anyone else. When she needs him to pretend to be her boyfriend to keep her mother's high society matches at bay, he goes all in.

After a weeks of hijinks at her family's expense, the two soon realize, no one's faking a thing in this fake relationship.

And Darla Jones finally finds something that clicks.

DARLA

FOUR MONTHS AGO - SOHO

ADULTING IS A LOAD OF CRAP.

Growing up sucks. I'm not sure what I expected, but it certainly wasn't this. It's been two days since college graduation, and the pressure's on—no more hiding behind books. People expect me to make decisions and declarations of intent. They expect maturity.

No, thank you. *I'll pass.*

All that sounds far too stressful for a young girl making her way into the world.

Everyone expects me to select some random job I'll probably hate, then follow it up with a suitable marriage to a boring man who wants a boring wife to give him boring children and tell him boring things until we grow old and die.

As I said, it's a load of crap.

"Darla, what about this one? This one looks nice. The lady says it's the best one they have."

These two are the main culprits: my parents---David and Davina Jones.

Can you believe that? Somehow a guy named David found a

woman named Davina and lived happily ever after. It's nauseating. Revolting. They're two peas in a pretentious pod. *Everything needs to be the best.*

The Jones family needs to keep up appearances.

"Does it matter, Daddy?" I offer a one-shoulder shrug and listen to the saleswoman's honeyed voice rattle off features she's practiced a thousand times. My parents look to me for questions, but I've got nothing. It's an incredible camera, top of the line, best on the market, and all that jazz. But I've got a nice one already.

What will I do with two cameras?

There's no need to ask that question. That's like asking them why you need two cars. No one needs two cars. You buy them because you can. Period.

"Sweetheart, I want to get you a new bag. I hate the one you carry." Mom slams her stiletto on the carpet, expecting to hear a sound. The silence catches her by surprise.

"No, I love my bag. A girl in the Fashion Department made it for me. It's one of a kind." I flash an icy glare towards my father, who then casts a stern eye at my mother.

"Cool it, Davina. It's *her* bag. She gets to choose her own bag. When we go shopping for you, you'll get to select your own." His booming voice makes her bristle with indignation, but only momentarily. Any proper punishment gets doled out behind closed doors. The pair are insufferable nymphomaniacs.

"But David... that bag!" She pushes, whining while she points to a bag I'm not actually carrying at the moment.

"What did I say?" He lifts one eyebrow and discreetly mocks a spanking motion. She yelps, pipes down, then giggles with delight.

Unbelievable.

"Sir? Lenses?" Fortunately for everyone, the saleswoman interrupts their sick love fest.

"Ah, yes. Darla, which lenses do you need?" He turns to the

woman. "My youngest daughter here just graduated from the School of Visual Arts. We're incredibly proud of her. She's going to be a photographer--- isn't that something? We need an artist in the family." He gives me a side hug and crushes me into his ribs.

She smiles sweetly and places six prime lenses on the counter. My face heats under the woman's gaze. No doubt she thinks I'm a brat. Mom looks like a million bucks in her Chanel and Cartier diamonds. Dad looks dapper in his Burberry suit. And their ridiculous daughter is sporting platform Converse, a white miniskirt, a retro white tube top, and a snazzy lime-green bolero jacket I found on consignment.

It's not like I don't own better clothes. My mother and grand-mother send me clothes every chance they get. It's their way of helping me fit into their world---the one I was born into. The one I'll never escape.

And why would I want to?

All that money. *All those expectations.*

I know I should be grateful. It comes with all the luxuries of life, and I don't want for anything. There's just something about it that doesn't sit well in my soul.

Something that doesn't click.

Maybe I ask for too much. *Perhaps I am a brat.*

I take a deep breath and point to three lenses, the 18, 35, and 100mm. "Those are the ones I'm missing, Daddy. That'll do for now."

"Are you sure, pumpkin? No zooms? No lights?" He points to equipment on the other side of the room and delights the sales-woman in front of us.

"Nope. I'm good. You know how much I hate clutter. We can come back for lights when I set up a studio. I'm not there yet." With a few words, I burst her bubble and ruin what might have been a sizable commission. Crafty as shit, she wastes no time correcting my mistake.

"Sir, why don't you purchase a gift card? It allows your

daughter to return on her own without hesitating to ask." She whips out a shiny box, shoves it in my father's beguiled face, and smiles from ear to ear.

He's such a sucker.

"Dad, you don't..." My words fall on deaf ears.

"Darla, darling, go stand with your mother. I don't want you to see the amount. It's a surprise." He beams and nudges me with his elbow. I wish he wouldn't. As much as I love photography, I'm not sure this is what I want to do with my life. But it's hard to get mad when he wants to play Santa Claus.

"Come here, sweetheart. Let your Dad have fun. You know how excited he gets buying gifts." Mom retrieves a tiny brush from her purse and proceeds to comb my tangled ponytail. She's not the most maternal woman in the world, but she's got her moments.

Yesterday's graduation tipped the scales. Mom wasn't expecting to break out a hankie when I walked the stage. It caught her as much as everyone else by surprise.

The School of Visual Arts was her idea. It's her alma mater. She studied interior design but never went into business. Dad knocked her up with my brother Denver the second they were married, and she claims he expected her to stay home and be a housewife.

I don't believe her. My brother was born in the late eighties, not in the fifties.

I don't know if she had higher aspirations. She conformed to her family's expectations, and eventually, they became her own. Mom was born into old money, and the women in her family become ladies of leisure. It's their birthright.

I stare at my reflection in the glass display case and notice my mother's heavy-handed brushing has pushed my ponytail off-center. I discreetly straighten it and sweep a few lingering strands off my face. There's nothing about me that resembles a lady of leisure. Those women are elegant and poised, like my sister

Demeter. She looks like Mom and the rest of the van der Beek women---tall, honey-blonde hair and legs for days.

I'm all Jones. Jones women are known for four things.

Enormous eyes. *Check.*

Small stature. *Check.*

Big boobs. *Check.*

And last but not least, auburn hair. *Check.*

My skanky sister looks like a runway model, and I look like a busty leprechaun with gigantic eyes. I'm a freak.

Is it any wonder I'm still a virgin?

No, I'm not cut out for this *lady of leisure* business. I'll make my own way in this world. I might not figure it out today or tomorrow.

But one day soon, I'll find something that clicks.

I know it's out there. *It's gotta be.*

TWO

DARLA

TWO WEEKS LATER- UPPER EAST SIDE

"Demi, are you sure about this? You don't have to decide right away. Your mother and I didn't even know you, and he were an item." Beads of sweat gather on my father's temples and cascade into his collar. The room can't be over seventy-two degrees, but he's a hot mess. My mother and I huddle together, shivering under her cashmere throw as we listen with ears perked to this unfolding scandal. This one's a doozy.

Demeter stands ready for the fight of her life, and she's as cool as a cucumber.

"I'm certain, Daddy. I've made up my mind, I'm marrying Angus. He plans to stop by in an hour to ask for my hand, but I thought it best if we spoke first." My sister speaks without a hint of remorse. Her confident tone seems slightly out of place. You don't tell your father you plan to marry one of his oldest friends without so much as a teensy bit of shame. I know I wouldn't. The mere thought makes my cheeks heat.

While she states her case, a hundred creepy thoughts flash through my mind. Agnus McNeill knew us as little girls. This feels incredibly salacious. He would have been my godfather if he wasn't Presbyterian.

Good heavens, he's Presbyterian. That won't go over well with Nana. And he's newly divorced---*that's strike two.*

My father's sweating continues. His handsome face turns beet red as he tries to loosen his tie and piece together some type of reply. His lips part, his mouth moves, but no words form. *Poor Daddy.*

Demeter offers no comfort. She sits idly by while the man who raised her strips off his jacket and kicks off his loafers in a desperate attempt to release the valve. This can't be good for his blood pressure.

"Mom, say something before he has a stroke," I whisper under the blanket.

"I don't know what to..." She murmurs, afraid of my sister's wrath. They've always been close, but I could tell today's announcement caught her by surprise. The one saving grace in my mother's eyes is that Angus is richer than God. She might forgive everything else if he can provide well for my sister.

"Say something, honey." She taps my arm.

"Me?"

"Go on. Before Demeter kills him."

My daughterly instinct kicks in. "Angus MacNeil is practically Daddy's age! For crying out loud, Demeter, we called him Uncle Angus for years! You could have given him a little warning." I swing my legs off the couch and rush to my father's side.

My support gives him the strength to find his voice. "Demi, what's gotten into you? Have you lost your mind? Why would you want to marry a man only five years younger than your father? It's obscene."

I hold my hands at my hips and stand defiantly in front of my Dad. "For the money---why else? Uncle Angus is the richest man we know. Demeter wants to be the wealthiest woman in New York, and if it means lying down with a shriveled up old man, she'll hold her nose and do it." I'm harsher than I need to be, and I fill my accusations with half-truths.

I haven't called Angus, *Uncle Angus,* since junior high. And he's hardly a shriveled-up old man. He's devastatingly handsome with the rock-hard body of a man in his thirties. I'm just babbling for my father's sake.

Demeter flies to her feet and sticks her bony finger into my chest. "Shut your mouth, twerp! What do you know about love? You haven't had a man since age fifteen when Michael Fitzsimmons dumped you for your best friend."

I gasp and fall into my father's sweaty chest, then promptly recoil with a shudder. "He did not dump me! I dumped him!" I can't believe my teenage love life has become fodder for consumption. "Oh, the hell with you. Marry your decrepit old man and have his old babies. See if I care." I yank my jean jacket from under my mother's legs and storm towards the foyer.

"Sweetheart, don't leave!" My father calls after me, but I'm too furious to stop. I need out of this freezing house. I need to breathe fresh air before I scream. The walls are closing in on me.

Everyone in this house knows I dumped Michael Fitzsimmons. Yes, he cheated on me with Phillipa Anders. Yes, I caught them red-handed on her stoop. But that piece of filth begged me back, and I declined. Demeter conveniently forgot to mention that part of the story.

Wretched gold-digging tramp.

"Hey, Darla!" Startling me out of my rage, my sister's partner in crime appears. Lana Howard, her best friend, and my some-time nemesis, appears from the guest bathroom dressed in head-to-toe pink. Combined with her cheerful disposition, she shocks my senses. Her whole ensemble is entirely too over-the-top for someone pushing twenty-six.

"So, what's the big news, Squirt? Your mom text me 9-11, but she didn't say why. Did something happen? Why are you leaving?" My eyes narrow, and her chipper disposition fades.

"Don't call me Squirt. I'm twenty-two." I snap and point to the door.

"Good luck. I'm out. Demeter just told everyone she's marrying Angus MacNeil. It's disgusting. Daddy might need medical attention." I weave past her, but she hooks her elbow into mine and stops me in my tracks.

Her horror is palpable. "Marrying Angus MacNeil? Demeter and Angus?" Her green eyes shoot out of their sockets. For once in her life, she's oblivious. Lana Howard, matchmaker extraordinaire, the queen of romance, had no clue her best friend was hooking up with shipping tycoon Angus MacNeil. How humiliating. Serves her right for being such a busybody.

"Unhand me, madame." I shake her off with no small degree of sass. Although she's changed for the better over the years, I won't forget the incessant teasing I endured when she and Demeter were know-it-all teenagers.

"Cut it out, Darla. Are you fucking serious? Demeter's marrying Angus MacNeil? He's fifty! He's got an ex-wife and grown children. What the hell is she thinking? She was too embarrassed to go public with their relationship, but now she's marrying him---that's preposterous. What reason could she have for marrying a man that age?" Six inches taller than me, she reaches over my head with ease and grabs her pale pink cardigan off the hook by the door.

"You know what she's thinking. She's got thirty billion reasons to marry him." Frustrated with the topic, I shake my head and reach for the doorknob. "It doesn't matter. Go talk to her yourself. If Demeter wants to marry an old man, that's on her. I wash my hands of this whole business." I swipe my palms back and forth and cross the threshold.

Two steps out, and I feel a heavy presence over my shoulder. I'm being followed. "Where do you think you're going?"

"With you. I'm not going in there. I want no part in this." She wrinkles her nose and crosses her arms defiantly. I hop down to the top of the stoop, and she jumps next to me, mimicking my posture. Another step and she repeats her moves with a smile. "Come on, Darla. Let's grab a coffee. I'll text Demeter and ask her for an explanation. You're right, it's her life, but I don't approve of anyone marrying for money."

"I don't drink coffee. Besides, I should head back to Brooklyn. I'm helping my Aunt Daisy's lawyer catalog her estate. She requested her artwork be split and donated to the Guggenheim and Brooklyn Museum. I'm saying goodbye and wrapping them up tonight." I breathe a heavy sigh and lift my wrist to check the time. I bet that old broad would have laughed out loud with this gossip. She always said Demeter lacked scruples.

"Sorry about your Aunt Daisy. I haven't seen you since her funeral." Lana leans in and lets her hands fall on my shoulders. "Listen, I don't like coffee either. But I do love hot tea. Let me buy you a hot chocolate, and we can spend thirty minutes talking shit about Demeter or whatever topic you like."

Uncomfortable with her familiarity, I wiggle my shoulders and free them from her grip. "Hot chocolate?"

"Hot chocolate."

"With whipped cream?" I ask, then hop down two steps.

"Of course. Give me forty minutes, and I'll throw in a pastry." She prances past me.

"Darla!" My big brother's disembodied voice appears. I look from side to side, then glance back to Lana, who meets me with the same befuddled stare.

"Denver?"

"Dolly! Over here!" He calls again. I shield my eyes to cover the glare of the sun and gaze across the street. And that's when I see him. Not Denver. *Who cares about my brother?* I see him all the time.

Standing next to him in all his scrumptious glory is none other than the divine Mr. Oscar Brennan.

Be still my heart.

My brother's best friend from college, my first real crush, and the only man I've ever loved, Oscar Edward Brennan, appears like a long-lost dream floating on a cloud across Park Avenue.

Dear Lord, I've died and gone to heaven.

"Hey Darla Jones, look at you. All grown up." The familiar voice that's often visited me in my dreams curls around my heart like a boa constrictor. I'll never shake him off again.

Did he say Darla Jones? He remembers my name. *Oh, my God!* Oscar remembers my name. The lightbulb explodes. Of course, he remembers your name, dummy. Your brother just used it seconds ago.

While I wait with hopeful expectations of marriage, three babies, and two dogs, he steps onto my stoop and lifts those steely blue eyes to mine.

I'm dead. *No, seriously.* Dead as a doornail. The last time was just a practice run.

He takes my hand in his, swaddling it with care in the most masculine hands I've ever felt. My knees tremble and weaken. I'm so overcome. I fear I'll swoon clean off these steps and break my nose on the pavement.

"Steady, girl," Lana whispers under her breath and clutches the back of my jacket for good measure.

I can't help myself. It's been seven long years since Oscar Brennan's long legs and big ears turned my world upside down. To my fifteen-year-old heart, he was a god among men. He was an Adonis from the wrong side of the tracks who came into my world and swept me off my feet. I felt desperate for him to carry me to the place that made him so rough around the edges.

After the Michael Fitzsimmons fiasco, I swore I'd give it all up to be Mrs. Brennan.

But then he disappeared. My teen heart broke. Hope faded to dust. And I resigned myself to live a lonely Oscar-less life forever---until now. After all this time, Oscar's here. Where has he been?

This is too good to be true.

I discreetly pinch my arm. Nope. I'm not dreaming.

"Why are you two out here? We were about to sit down for dinner when Mom text me with 9-11. What the hell's going on?" Denver speaks words that go in one ear and out the other. He's got nuisance questions I can't answer. All I can do is stare at the beautiful man standing less than a foot away.

Why is he standing so close?

"I hope nothing happened to you." Oscar offers a devilish grin, and my heart dances a tiny jig.

"No, I'm fine... It was my... I mean, it is..." I press my hands against my flushed cheeks and feel them grow warm under his gaze. I can't remember the meaning of words. I've forgotten how to speak and breathe.

What am I saying?

Where am I?

Who am I?

"Dolly!" Denver waves his hand in front of my face. "Stop making eyes at Oscar and tell me what's going on."

I startle with horror---too much horror to answer. Of all the two-bit lousy things to do to your little sister. Shame washes over me and coils into the depths of my roiling tummy.

Denver Jasper Jones, I curse you. I curse you straight to hell. You will rue this day until your bloated gnarled body washes up on the shore of the East River and snakes...

"Denver Jones, you watch your mouth! She's not making eyes at anyone. Darla isn't feeling well. That's why I'm taking her out of here and dragging her away for some soup. You better apologize this instant." Lana saves the day and prevents me from summoning the forces of evil to murder Denver in his sleep.

"Sorry, Darla." He shifts his beady eyes to Oscar, then back to me. Denver doesn't buy it for a second, but he wants answers, and he's too hard up for Lana to call her a liar. "Will someone please tell me what we're heading into?"

"It's Demeter. She just informed everyone she's marrying

Angus MacNeil. You better get inside and calm Daddy down before Angus arrives." I wave a thumb at the front door and let one eye stray to Oscar.

Oh, wow. Is he ogling? I know I'm not imagining it. *Am I imagining it?*

This is no time to doubt myself. I clasp my hands under my chest to steady my limbs and give my breasts a gentle lift, offering a tiny incentive in their direction. I may not have much experience reading men, but I know when someone's undressing me with their eyes.

Denver notices too. A sharp elbow to Oscar's ribs breaks his focus and ruins our beautiful moment. "Angus McNeil? Dad's best friend?"

My brother bares his teeth and clenches his fists at his sides. "That old man better not show his face here. Come on, Oscar." Denver's growl sounds like the hiss of an annoyed tabby. My brother doesn't know the first thing about fighting. He grew up with sisters and would probably slap and kick if things got ugly.

"Good luck." I laugh as I make my way down the stoop. "Make sure not to tuck your thumb into your fist, or you'll break it."

Oscar, who hasn't said a word since Denver accused me of flirting, finally speaks up. "Hey man, I shouldn't be here. This is personal family shit, and the last thing I want to do is get in Angus MacNeil's crosshairs. I'm heading home. Call me tomorrow." He bounds towards the street before my brother drags him inside.

Frustrated by this abandonment, Denver waves him off and storms through the front door. I don't know why my mother called him. He'll only make things worse. As much as I love my older brother, he's a bit of a hothead who's all bark and no bite. He'll rile everyone up and then slink away when it gets too hot to handle. No doubt Oscar considered these facts when he made his stealthy retreat.

Eager to creep away, I duck my head and dash towards the crosswalk. I can't bear any further humiliations. We had our steamy interlude, exchanged a few heated glances under the twilight sky, and now I can carry those sweet memories for years to come.

There's no need to inject hope where there's none.

When I reach the intersection, I tap the crosswalk button and turn to look for Lana. My eyes flare, stunned by the sight heading my way.

"Lana said you wouldn't mind if I joined you for soup. She said you're heading to Brooklyn after dinner. I live in Brooklyn. Is it okay if I tag along?" Oscar offers a crooked smile, and hordes of butterflies take flight.

"You don't mind, do you? He lives in Park Slope too. Isn't that a coincidence?" Lana winks and gives me a thumbs-up behind his back.

"No, I don't mind at all."

THREE

OSCAR

TWO WEEKS LATER- BROOKLYN

I love New York, but I hate Manhattan.

It's the land of social climbers. People with no souls and hearts will happily sell out their grandmothers for a shot at the brass rings. Everyone wants to be something they're not. Everyone wants to keep up with the Jones's.

It's not for me.

I like who I am. I might not be much, but I'm comfortable in my own skin, and I don't cringe when I stare at my reflection in the mirror. Few attorneys can say the same.

I didn't have the easiest time growing up. My dad died in a car accident a few months before I was born. It hit my mom pretty hard. When you become a widow at twenty-three, everyone expects you to remarry. They told her to do it for me. Then they pushed her to do it for her as if she didn't know her own mind.

She always swore my father's love was enough to last her a lifetime. She often said, "His love filled so much space in my heart. There's only room leftover for you."

Maybe a part of her knew she wouldn't be here long enough for another love.

When I was twenty-four, she discovered the back pain bugging her for years was stage three pancreatic cancer.

I didn't know—- I wasn't here. Stuck in Boston with my head buried in law books, I was halfway through my second year at Harvard Law when she was first diagnosed. I saw her over Easter, and she looked thinner, but she dismissed my worries. She changed the subject and prattled on about getting back on her *Jenny Craig* diet. I should have known better, but law school left me so brain-fried, I didn't know my ass from my elbow.

Mom didn't make it easy and worked overtime to keep me in the dark. She knew how hard I worked to get into Harvard and what my scholarship meant for my future. But there was nothing more important than her.

She suffered in silence. She needed me, and I wasn't here for her. I'll never forgive myself, and I'll never get back the year I lost.

That summer, she progressed into stage four. I gave up my scholarship and transferred to NYU. It broke her heart, but there was no fucking way I could leave her alone in Brooklyn and head back to Boston like a fool without a mother.

There's no way I'd give up the last months of her life. We'd always been a team. Me and her. She and me. Through thick and thin until the end.

She made it through Christmas but never saw the New Year. I miss her every day, and I try to be the person she wanted me to be.

Be the kind of lawyer who helps the little guy.
No one ever looks out for the little guy.

Transferring to NYU cost me time and money. You don't get scholarships in your third year of law school. I graduated a year late and went into debt doing it. Staring down the barrel of a thirty-year student loan, I felt forced to sell my mother's home in

Bay Ridge and take an apartment in Park Slope. It's a friendlier neighborhood and closer to lower Manhattan.

I know I hate Manhattan, but I need to work, and I'm lucky enough to have brilliant partners who believe in the importance of real pro-bono work.

Fallon, Renaldi & Brennan, LLP has a nice ring to it. I know that sounds simple, but it took us a long time to come up with the name. We fought for days about the order of our names. We're attorneys--- it's what we do.

Harper Fallon and I come from the same neighborhood in Brooklyn. We're both Irish and raised by single moms. But her old man is still alive, and he's someone big. He throws money at her and sends lawyers to give her what she's owed, but she won't talk to him. It's a sore spot, so I don't bring it up.

She handles most of the civil cases but specializes in divorce. We may work in Soho, but women travel from all over Manhattan to retain her services. She's a shark in court.

Andrea Renaldi specializes in Immigration and Civil Rights. She had less experience than Harper and I, but her father gave us the seed money to get started, and she proved herself by landing us a Supreme Court case our first year in business.

She looks like Nicole Kidman's sexy Italian cousin, but she's a fierce and unwavering advocate for her clients. She's also really fussy about the way you pronounce her first name. It's *Ahn-dray-ah*, not *Ann-dree-a*.

God help you if you say it wrong.

We found each other at our last gig, the New York County Public Defender's Service, and set up shop three years ago. I had other offers, some far more lucrative, but this one felt best. It's never been about the money to me. I promised my Mom I'd help the little guy, and I can't let her down.

I don't give a fuck about keeping up with the Jones's. I've known that family for years, and there's nothing special about their world.

Denver Jones and I met on our first day at Harvard. People think he's a prick, but after ten years, he's become one of my closest friends. He could have been a pompous dick like the rest of his Park Avenue buddies, but he's always been cool with me. For all his money, he might be the most miserable guy I know.

Everyone thinks money makes your life easy.

Not this kind of money. Too much makes it a nightmare.

Denver's life was settled the moment his parents found out they were having a boy. After he attended the best day school, he was shipped off to a top-notch prep school. Yale preceded Harvard Law, and finally, they squeezed him into a position at his grandfather's firm.

Poor guy never wanted to become a lawyer. He's got a big heart and wants to do right by his family, but he still hasn't figured out his way in the world. Somewhere deep inside, an artist is dying to come out. But someone has to take over when his father retires, and all arrows point to him.

As close as I am to Denver, I've kept my distance from the other Jones's. Obscene wealth makes me uncomfortable. I was born and raised in New York City, but two minutes in their living room and I feel like Jed Clampett from the *Beverly Hillbillies.* It's nothing overt, but I know how to read a room.

The dad's not so bad, just a little pushy. Every time I see him, he tries to hire me. The Jones Family firm needs litigators. The prep-school chums they employ have spent their careers avoiding the inside of a courtroom, and that's the one place I shine.

I could make a nice chunk of change working for David Jones, but I've no interest in being a corporate attorney. *That's not my style.*

The mom's nice to my face, but deep down, she's an incurable snob. She always feared I'd make a play for her daughter, Demeter, and sully their family name. The thought makes me laugh.

I'd sooner become a priest.

There are few women capable of turning me off more than Demeter Jones. If a gust of hot wind accidentally got me hard, she'd have me flaccid in seconds. She's one of the worst people I've ever met.

"What can I get you?" The barista stares me down from the opposite end of the counter while the long line of angry customers glares at me with muted contempt. I've hesitated no longer than thirty seconds.

Sometimes I hate this fucking city.

"Get me a latte with skim and a hot chocolate with two percent, extra whipped cream, to go." I bark my order and hold out my phone for zapping.

"Hot chocolate?" I'm greeted by judgment.

"Did I stutter?" I wave my phone to get his attention. He quirks a bushy eyebrow and lifts his wand to zap the code on my screen. The line grows restless.

"Dude, it's July." He turns as he mumbles his smart-ass comment.

"How hot is my fucking coffee? Mind your own damn business. It's for my girl. She hates coffee." I shift to the left to let the following person order but watch the jerk with eyes like a hawk in case there's any funny business. I don't need him taking my sass out on Darla's chocolate.

Four minutes later, I'm out the door.

Darla Jones isn't my girl. I'm not sure what she is. She's Denver's baby sister, but now we're friends. Good friends... maybe... I think.

I take the crosswalk across Flatbush and head down 8th Avenue.

She's a little adorable, nothing like Demeter, inside or out. Too rich for my blood. But there's something about her that keeps me coming back for more. I wish I could put it into words. I think if I could label it, I might get her out of my system before it's too late.

I've got no business getting hot and bothered over Denver's kid sister. She's the sister he likes. This is the sister no one will ever be good enough to marry.

Why did I say marry?

I'm talking out of my ass. I mean, Denver already thinks we spend too much time together, and it won't get any better after today. Darla's becoming the girl next door. Literally. Okay, not literally. She'll be three houses away.

Isn't that weird? Not weird as in *bad*. Weird as in *cool*.

Her Great Aunt Daisy, a cheeky old broad I met half a dozen times on my morning run and whom I had no idea she was related to the Jones clan, left her a six-bedroom, 5,800 square-foot Neo-Grecian style four-story brownstone worth over five million dollars. *Can you believe that?* That's fucking incredible. And she's moving in today.

No one will be pleased. Least of all, Darla's mother. The Jones's don't live in Brooklyn. They're Upper Manhattan people. Anything below 59th Street is unsuitable.

I'm heading over now for moral support. Darla loved her aunt, and her aunt wanted her to live in it. I kind of like the idea of having her close. I think Brooklyn suits her. She's meant for different things or a different sort of life. She's a little clueless about the world, but she's got a good heart, and those giant blue eyes give me a warm fuzzy feeling.

"Hey, kiddo. I brought your chocolate." I ignore the small crowd of yapping prima donnas chewing her ear off and hand her a tall cup of hot chocolate, extra whipped cream with two shakes of cinnamon. Just the way she likes it.

"Oscar! You made it!" Her dark expression disappears. Dark pink lips curve into a silly grin as she twists off the lid and examines the contents. Her eyes brighten. "Oh, my goodness. You remembered my cinnamon. I'm not going to find an engagement ring at the bottom, am I?" She sinks her teeth into her bottom lip and giggles.

"Stop that," Denver growls, then punches my shoulder. "Why are you buying her chocolate? This feels sexual. Are you boning my sister?"

Darla gasps and nearly spits out her first sip.

"Denver! What's wrong with you? They're friends. You're just friends, aren't you?" Mrs. Jones tries to make light of an awkward situation, but her voice trembles with concern.

"Everyone shut up! You're humiliating me!" Darla stomps her foot and shouts at the top of her lungs.

"What are we waiting for? Wasn't the realtor meeting us here?" Denver looks from side to side. His eyes grow suspicious. "Hey Dolly, when is he meeting us? We're just doing a run-through, right? We need to get going before traffic gets heavy on the Long Island Express."

Darla's eyes flash to mine, and we exchange a nod. *It's going down.*

Nana Junie, Darla's paternal grandmother, lifts her sunglasses to her face, taps her purse like she's assuring us she's armed, and gives her granddaughter a discreet thumbs-up. She bankrolled the renovations on the sly and kept Darla's secret. I'm uncertain if she approves of the location, but Darla's the apple of her grandparent's eye, and whatever she wants, she gets.

I'm discovering that about her.

Darla clears her throat. "Mom, Dad, Denver... there's no easy way to say this, so I'll rip the band-aid in one yank. There's no realtor. I'm not going to the Hamptons this weekend, and I'm not selling." She takes a deep breath and pauses for effect. "I'm moving in."

"Darla! No!" Mrs. Jones sucks in a sharp breath, fans herself, then swoons into her husband's chest. Too dazed to gauge the severity of his wife's reaction, Mr. Jones fails to extend his arms, and her limp body falls to the sidewalk headfirst.

If she wasn't out before, she is now.

One by one, we cast our eyes to the ground and stare at the

crumpled mess splayed clumsily in her couture sundress and espadrille wedges.

Denver speaks first. "I hope you're happy, Dolly. You've killed Mom."

FOUR

DARLA

FIVE MINUTES LATER-BROOKLYN

"Say something, David. Say something before I do." My hysterical mother scrambles to her knees and uses my father's legs to pull herself back onto her Gucci espadrilles. They're new. She'll never forgive herself if she scuffs them before their proper debut in East Hampton.

"Darla, are you sure? It's a long way from home, sweetie." Daddy searches my face for a glimmer of doubt. When he doesn't find any, he turns to his mother, Nana Junie.

"It's only twelve miles, and this is the best neighborhood in Brooklyn. Come inside and see what we've done to the house. Don't disappoint your daughter, David." She squints and taps her purse. That's her signal. Heed her warning, or she'll call Papa Desmond---the man in charge.

He takes a step back and helps my mother brush off her clothes. He's familiar with her warnings. The last time she tapped her purse and followed through, she changed her will and left his favorite family home in Rye, overlooking Long Island Sound, to me.

That was harsh.

"I know it's a big step. But I promise I'm ready." I stand my ground, then take this golden opportunity to lean ever so casually against Oscar. He holds steady and welcomes the weight of my body. It's a shameless act of a desperate woman, but one I hope goes unnoticed by these killjoys.

He's got sixteen inches on me---6'5 to my 5'1. It's not surprising when my shoulder blades tuck perfectly against the sculpted grooves of his finely tuned ab muscles. His t-shirt is so thin I'm positive I can make out all six, or do I feel eight?

Eight? *Damn, that's hot.*

"I see you, Dolly." Denver digs his fingers into my shoulders and jerks me away from Oscar's cozy warmth. "You can't move out here by yourself. It may look nice in the day, but you're a young woman living alone. What if something happens to you? It would take forever for one of us to get to you."

I squirm out of his grasp and bound up my stoop, seeking refuge behind my Nana, *the enforcer.* "I'm twenty-two years old. That's the same age you were when you moved to Boston. Brooklyn's a whole hell of a lot closer than Boston. Stop treating me like a baby. This house is perfect. Nana Junie went to town on the renovations. She had her guys build me a freaking studio and an office for my photography business."

"What business?!" Denver rudely interrupts.

"Shut it." Nana lowers her sunglasses and frowns. "She graduated last month. Give her a break. Your grandfather loves her composition. She's going to be famous!"

My mother can't take another second of Nana's encroachment. She grabs my father by his lapels and shakes him. "Damn it, David! Do something! Your mother is stealing my baby again."

"Davina, you know Mom loves Darla like she's her own. She's only trying to help. Why don't we see the house? Darla's put a lot of work into this, sweetheart." Dad tries to comfort her with a kiss on her forehead, but his answer clearly deflates her spirits.

She nods and shuffles her feet towards the stoop. "I'm not happy about this, Dolly." Her misty eyes shift to mine as she bites down on her quivering lip. "You should know you're killing your mother by degrees."

Nana Junie clears her throat and claps the tip of her palm. "That's enough. It's time for the big reveal. Please proceed, milady." She smiles and curls her hand like a game show hostess, gesturing for me to lead everyone up the stoop.

"I need a moment to take this in."

"Take your time, darling." She whispers. In the distance, I hear my mother's mumbled curses and try to push them out of my mind.

It's not every day you move into your first house.

I draw a deep breath and drop my gaze to the envelope in my hands. I peel it open and remove the neatly furled batch of papers. My heart pounds as I unfold the contents, and the crisp white sheets catch on my fingers. A bead of sweat trickles down my spine. I lift them up against the sun and stare with wide-eyed wonder at my name on the deed.

Darla Juniper Jones.

Oscar snaps a photo right on cue. Nana Junie claps with enthusiasm.

"What if something happens to you? How could I go on living if something happens to my baby?" Mom skitters up the steps and blocks my path.

"Mom! You're ruining my independent woman photo. Please clear the stoop." I flap my hand then turn to Oscar. "You promised you wouldn't laugh, right?"

He brandishes his phone. "I'm here to catalog the event. No laughing."

"Nana? Did you bring it?"

Nana Junie reaches into her tote and hands me her blue-knit striped beret from the seventies. It's fresh from the cleaners, just like she promised. I drop my ponytail and shake out my hair.

While my brother and parents look on in utter amazement, I pull it onto my head and tilt it to the side, just like Mary Richards wore it in the Mary Tyler Moore Show.

"Are you serious, Dolly?" Denver laughs and tries to shame me into taking it off. But the way I see it, we get one life. No matter how silly we feel, some things are worth doing.

"Leave her alone. She's thought about it for days." Oscar defends me and lifts his phone to start filming. "Ready when you are."

"Nana?"

She taps a button on her phone, and the final forty-five seconds of Mary's theme music chime forth.

"Action!" When Oscar barks his commands, I sprint to the top of the stoop, spin, and throw my hat in the air.

"And cut!"

"That was perfect, baby!" Nana shakes her fists like a pair of maracas.

Oscar gives me a thumbs up.

Mom is livid.

"Are you sure, honey?" Dad does his best to appear upbeat.

"I think I'll be happy here..." My words trickle off the beaten path, and I take in the gravity of these next few steps. This could be the house where I raise my babies. Maybe my husband and I will live our lives here. One day we'll retire and sit by my bay windows, sipping coffee and complaining how the neighborhood isn't what it used to be. I can picture it now.

There's something here that breeds a hopeful outlook. I can feel it in the air. There's no way to put it into words, but it's sizzling. It feels like something's just around the corner. It's stumbling towards me, and there's nothing I can do to stop it.

It's the darnedest feeling.

"What are you waiting for?" My mother nudges me forward and sulks. "Let's see it. Your father and I need to get on the road."

"Hush up. It's a big deal to open your door on moving day." I close my eyes and touch the glass inlay mahogany French doors. Giddy with excitement, I run my fingers along the decorative trim and marvel at the detail. They're breathtaking. The artisan Papa Desmond hired worked overtime to meet my specifications, but I never expected this level of craftsmanship.

"Come on, Dolly. You know how bad the holiday traffic gets---move it along." Denver obliterates another tender moment when he tries to yank the keys out of my hand.

Mom seizes her chance to speak her peace. "You're twenty-two years old and not street smart enough to handle the tough streets of Brooklyn, little girl. You'll be all alone!"

"Tough streets? My sister-in-law loved her neighborhood. It's one of the nicest in the city." Nana sucks the wind from her sails, then lifts her phone and angles it towards me. "Go on, sweetie."

Lost in a daze of emotion, I slide the key into the keyhole and release a slow breath. A soft squeal escapes at the sound of the click. My heart thumps loudly in my ears.

"Here goes!" I push the door a few inches, then trip over my feet when I hear the sound of Oscar's voice.

"You don't have to worry about her being alone. I'm three houses down. If she needs anything, I'm a quick phone call away." His sweet words sink deep into my soul and warm my heart.

"I'll take good care of her."

And with those words, my heart explodes clear out of my chest and lands somewhere in the foyer.

Yes, please, take care of me.

"Son of a bitch! I knew it!" As I take that monumental first step into my new home, I hear Denver fly across the porch and tackle Oscar.

Hackles rise. Fur flies. Oscar grunts. A deep dark place inside of me thrills. I hear a feminine slap, presumably from my brother, before his high-pitched scream pierces my ears.

Fortunately, it's over as soon as it starts. Oscar quickly over-powers my brother before his cheap shot sends them rolling down the stoop.

"Goddamn it, Denver!"

Nana Junie dives into her purse. "Don't worry, darling. I'll call your granddaddy."

FIVE

OSCAR

TWO MONTHS LATER- BROOKLYN

"No more, Oscar. I can't take it. My legs feel like Jello."

Darla skitters to a stop and wobbles into my chest, clutching my shoulders for dear life. I wrap my arm around her waist and savor a moment that never lasts long.

Huffing and panting, she drags her weary limbs onto her stoop and reclines her sweaty body across three rows of steps. Her wet running shirt clings to her breasts. The running shorts that make my pulse spiral out of control every damn time she overtakes me on our morning run are soaked through with perspiration.

My lusty gaze settles on the cleft between her thighs. It leaves nothing to the imagination, but that doesn't keep me from imagining more. I can't help myself. Darla's a miniature Coke bottle with sharp angles and cushy little curves.

I don't know what I did to deserve this type of torture.

God knows I've tried to be good. Apart from my active flirtation with my best friend's baby sister, I live like a fucking monk.

Dazed and exhausted, I stagger behind then tap the timer on

my watch. "5.5 miles. That's a record for us." I nudge into her, and we sit bicep to bicep. "Scoot over, Jones."

She frowns, then wiggles her ass a few inches to the right. "I've got twelve steps on this stoop, Brennan. I don't know why you need to plant your stinky behind right next to me." She elbows my rib. "Don't get too close. I'm sure I reek, and I'll die if you get a whiff of my pits."

I lean closer and take a generous sniff. My mouth floods. If it wasn't utterly inappropriate, I'd pull off Darla's shorts, rip off her top and run my tongue down every inch of her sweat-soaked body. "You smell fine. Grapefruit, lilac, and Darla sweat. They should bottle it and sell it at Saks..."

What am I saying?

Shut your goddamn mouth before you give yourself away.

Her body stiffens for a beat. It's almost imperceptible, but I catch it. She's on to me. She knows I'm a fucking stalker.

Stalker?

No, I'm not that bad. So, I read her shower gel ingredients. Believe me, I've done worse.

Do you hear yourself?

You're an officer of the court, sworn to protect the law, and you are days from breaking into this woman's home at night to watch her sleep.

Please, stop talking to yourself before she thinks you're crazy too.

"Did you hear me?" Darla slaps my thigh and jostles my attention back to her.

Her sky-blue eyes meet mine, and my heart skips a beat with each flutter of those long dark lashes. I can't keep this up. Next time I see Denver, I'll tell him I'm in love with his sister. Fuck him. Fuck his weird code. A man can only take so much.

No, I promised him I wasn't interested in his sister. If I bring it up, he'll just pick another fight, and the last time he broke his arm falling down Darla's stoop.

"Sorry, brain fog. I need water." I swallow hard and smack my lips as proof.

"I said, I quit this morning ritual. My feet look gross." She unties her laces, steps out of her sneakers, and pulls off her socks. I feast my eyes on her adorable little toes and imagine putting each one in my mouth. My cock twitches to life.

There's nothing gross about her feet---they could grace the cover of magazines. They're a foot fetishist wet dream. Not that I'd let any of those sick fucks anywhere near them.

"You push too hard, and I can't afford any blisters right now. In two weeks, my sister marries in an obnoxious wedding weekend blowout in Rye. All my dresses call for strappy heels. These puppies can't take much more abuse." She wiggles her toes then jumps to her feet, bending over to stretch her back.

The curve of her ass comes into view, and blood siphons south. I can't tell if she does it on purpose. It feels innocent, but she *must* know I like her. There's no way I've been slick enough to disguise my feelings. I'm a horrible actor.

"I'm sorry, you're right. I didn't mean to push so hard. You looked like you were on a roll." My racing heart skids into my sternum. There are so many ways I'd like to push her too hard, and not one fucking scenario involves running.

Another boner. *Shit.* It's been so long since I've had sex, I've lost the ability to control them. I shift back and forth and let my mind wander to anything but the here and now.

It's always the same whenever I'm around Darla. I fight tooth and nail to hold back an arousal that's as natural as the tides. She's beautiful. A pint-size goddess. And she's completely unaware of just how sexy she can be without even trying.

Stomping up her stoop, she struts defiantly on the cutest, shapeliest legs I've ever seen. I'm so screwed. Hard, screwed, and going out of my mind.

I don't know why Denver cares. We've been friends for ten years. He knows I'm not a philanderer. I work non-stop, and although I'll never have her kind of money, he knows I don't give a damn about shit like that.

If I wanted more money, I could make more money.

The truth is as plain as the big nose on my face. Denver doesn't think I'm good enough for his sister. Maybe he's right. But if you ask me, it's a dick move. I'm crazy about her. I'll worship the ground she walks on. No Park Avenue prick could ever treat her as good as me.

Ultimately, it's on me. Love this big doesn't happen every day. Instead of pouncing, wrestling her to the ground, and shoving my ring on her finger, I've been dawdling, twiddling my thumbs, and hoping our stars collide at just the right moment. But that's not the way love works.

"Are you coming?" Her voice calls like a siren song, and I drag my cowardly ass up the stoop, horrified by the size of my erection. I shift my cock as I walk, nearly punching it to make it go down.

"Are we still on for bowling tonight?" I remind her as we head into her kitchen. "Andrea's bringing our new team shirts and asked us to be there ten minutes early."

She offers me a glass of water and hums to herself. "Of course, we're on. I had the second-highest score." She wags her eyebrows and smiles. My heart melts and pools on the Spanish tile under my feet.

Fucking Denver. If it was anyone else, I'd tell them to go to hell and mind their own goddamn business. No one would stop me from taking what I want.

And I want Darla. *I really do.*

"Why don't we grab some lunch in the city? It's a beautiful September day. We can hang out in the park." My heart beats a mile a minute while I wait for her to reply. I think I just asked her for a date. We hang out daily, but my words came out differently this time. They feel different. Maybe it's all in my head.

Buzzing around the room, she appears unaffected by my

question. She removes an apple from a bowl by the sink, runs it under the faucet, then wipes it off with a dishrag. Before she lifts it to her mouth, her eyes drift to mine for a split second, then leave me hanging, torturing me with silence.

"Darla?" I check in.

"Oh, crap. I thought I answered you." She replies with a mouth full of apple. "I can't hang out today. My mother and sister are taking me to lunch. This is undoubtedly another of their traps, and bachelor number two will saunter by and join us just after they serve appetizers. They think they're so clever."

"What?" I blink in disbelief. "Bachelor number two? Who was bachelor number one?" My voice quivers like a teenage boy being dumped.

She swallows and continues. "Just some dandy who works with Dad and Denver...Orson Pierce...no, I'm sorry, Orson Pearson." She drains her glass of water and prances out of the kitchen, blissfully unaware she's just kicked me in the balls.

My eyes flare as I try to swallow the lump in my throat. Is Denver behind this? Is this the beginning of the end for us? Why would she agree to round two?

I follow her into the foyer, angry she's discounted me so quickly. I know I'm dragging my ass, but most of the time, she treats me like a eunuch.

"Why go if you suspect a trap?" I'm as surprised as she is when a low, raspy grumble emerges. I can't control the beat of my heart. My fingers itch to slide into those deep auburn locks, hold on tight and bring those sassy lips crashing into mine.

But what if she pushes me away? I might never get another chance.

She yawns, ignorant or indifferent to my heart tearing in two. "We need to discuss wedding stuff. Demeter's wedding is five weeks away, and this wedding weekend bullshit is proving to be a headache and a half. But it makes no difference. Bring on the bachelors. I can handle myself just fine." She waves her hand dismissively like she didn't just punch me in the gut.

What is she saying? Is that an admission? Did she just say she's going on a date? My eye twitches with muted rage.

My brain explodes. "Darla, we need to talk."

Offering no further details to ease my concern or provide an ounce of solace, she leads me towards the front door with nothing more than a smile and kick in her step.

I can't go yet. *Not yet.* I struggle to piece together words that will keep Darla here, safe with me and away from other men's prying eyes. Just because she rejected the other moron doesn't mean bachelor number two won't win her heart. Anything can happen. I'm not foolish enough to think Darla doesn't have urges. It's probably been months since she's been with...I can't finish the sentence. The thought turns my stomach.

When we reach the threshold, I turn to speak, but her tiny hand strikes my chest and hurls me onto the porch like I'm *Dennis the Menace.* "We'll talk tonight. I need to shower and put myself together. You know the way Demeter can be. They're sending a car in two hours, and I'm already behind. Come get me at 6:00. See ya!"

Before I can reply or say goodbye, she slams the door in my face.

I'm going to kill Denver.

SIX

OSCAR

LATER THAT DAY- SOHO

I NEARLY MISS MY STATION. THE TRAIN CLEARS, NEW PASSENGERS get on, and I'm too focused on the hundreds of faces, law school classmates with sinister grins and busy hands lining up to meet Darla for lunch today.

Men more suitable than me.

Orson Pearson doesn't just work with Denver. They've known one another since prep school. After they graduated from Yale, he followed him to Harvard Law. He's tried his entire life to join the Jones Family. Luckily, my Darla saw right through him.

But who's bachelor number two? Albert Reynolds? Pierre Bishop? Max Burns? Chase Weatherby? *That's such a stupid name.*

How many greedy blue-blooded philanderers will they line up before one finally piques Darla's interest? It's only a matter of time. She's a young woman. As much as I hate to admit it, Pierre's a charming guy. Maybe he'll be the one to coax my lady to the altar.

Sweet Jesus, I'll wring that Frenchie's neck. *Is he French?* Why would you name your kid Pierre if you're not French? It doesn't matter. He's a dead man.

As the doors slide to a close, I lift my eyes to the platform and read the sign hanging over the flock of commuters: *Broadway-LaFayette.* My brain clicks, my legs leap, and I almost catch my arm on the resealing doors. I've hardly got my bearings when the train accelerates out of the station into the tunnel.

Son of a bitch, that was a close one.

This won't work. If I'm going to confront Denver, I need to have my wits about me. He agreed to meet me for lunch in Soho. We met at a bar last week, and in typical fashion, I made no mention of Darla. All I wanted to do was talk about Darla, and I held back. I figured the less I say, the better. She's his baby sister. Guys don't like to hear about their friends getting together with their sisters---especially their little sisters.

But that was before I knew he was setting her up with other guys.

I won't stand for this. That prick won't pretend to be my friend for ten years, come to me with his bullshit problems, ask me to help him study for the Bar Exam, cry over wanting to be an artist and then look down his nose at me like I'm not good enough for his sister.

I stop on the corner of Houston and Lafayette and draw a deep breath of polluted air into my lungs. The sounds of the city reverberate in my brain and soothe my hackles. I'm in my element. If you grow up in the country, the sound of crickets might bring you peace. For me, it's the noise of the city. Honking cars, screeching tires, and feet pounding the hot pavement.

I follow a small group of tourists into the near-empty bistro and give them a moment to figure out their game plan. They speak in hushed tones, unsure if they want to eat here and decide to put it to a vote. My patience wears thin. When I sigh with exasperation, a young woman waves me ahead, and I weave past them towards the hostess stand.

"Reservation for two. Oscar Brennan."

"Your party's here. To the left, by the window, sir." She offers to lead me, but I shake my head and fly off.

I can do this. I've got nothing to lose and everything to gain.

All I want is the opportunity to woo her. He can say no. And I can tell him to go to hell. I value our friendship, but this could be bigger. This could be forever.

I'm an attorney, for fuck's sake. If anyone knows how to present a rational argument by highlighting key evidence, focusing on relevant facts, and minimizing emotion--- it's me. I argued a case in front of the Supreme Court and won. I helped create legislation. Do you really think I can't handle confronting my friend like a mature adult?

I turn the corner and spot Denver lounging in a booth by the window, without a care in the world. His eyes dart back and forth, eyeing the menu with greed while his fat mouth chugs his pretentious imported beer.

My fortitude dissolves.

"Hey, dickhead! Is this your fucking knife in my back?" I stomp down the crowded aisle and jerk my thumb over my shoulder.

He stares speechless, stunned by my accusation. "What the shit?"

I slide into the booth and fix my eyes on his. "Did you think I wouldn't find out?"

His brow creases. "Find out what? What did I do?" He tenses, then shifts his gaze from side to side, scanning his memories for anything that might fit the bill. "Help me out, jackass."

The server approaches. "Can I get you something to drink?"

"Brooklyn Lager. Thanks."

"Just tell me what the fuck I did so I can apologize. You know I wouldn't fuck you over on purpose." Denver lifts the menu to cover his face, then eases it down. "And who says I did anything? Why are you so quick to accuse your friend?"

I yank the menu out of his hands. "How's your arm, asshole?

Did you enjoy breaking it for nothing? I see you broke nothing when Orson tried to hook up with Darla?"

The server returns with my beer, pops off the tab, and offers a frosty glass. I wave my hand to decline and take the bottle. When I turn to Denver, his pale face greets me. His mouth parts, and his lip curls with disgust. His knuckles turn white as his hands ball into tight fists. "Darla? Orson? I didn't set them up. Are you fucking kidding me? That cretin? I don't want that pervert anywhere near Darla!" He lifts his arm and screams for the check. "I'm going to kill that son of a bitch."

I slap his arm with the menu. "Hold on, asshole. I'm starving, and I'm not done yet."

He sneers with irritation. "Hungry? I see that shithead every day. He has the balls to make a play for my sister and stay silent. I don't think so. When did this happen? Did Darla tell you?" He lifts his arm, and I hit it again.

"Cut your shit out. Are you straight with me? Because your mother and sister are probably rolling out bachelor number two at *Daniel's* as we speak." I search the menu for something to eat, then watch his face for signs of dishonesty.

His eyes glaze over. "Bachelor number two? What does that mean?"

Denver may be many things, but he's not much of a liar. He tries, but he gives himself away mid-sentence. He's not lying now. If his mother wants to find Darla a respectable boyfriend or husband, he's not privy to her schemes.

I take a swig of beer and set the bottle on the table. "That's what Darla calls them. She suspects your mother is trying to find her a man---a suitable man."

He shakes his head. "I'll put a stop to this bullshit. Darla's too young for that nonsense, and she's vulnerable prey for the guys from work. They know how much she's worth. They'd love to get their hands on her money."

His words leave a bitter taste in my mouth. He's not wrong

about those men, but Darla's so much more. "Your sister is beautiful. She's smart and funny. They may want more than her money. Is that what you think of me? Did you automatically assume I wanted your sister's money, dickhead?" I snarl and pound my fist on the table.

His brow furrows deep, and his gaze sharpens. "You? I thought I dealt with you. Are you messing around with my sister? No bullshit, Oscar. We're supposed to be friends. Friends don't fuck around with each other's sisters." He points his beer bottle at me then takes a drink.

My shoulders sag. I take a deep breath and exhale with aggravation. "I like your sister. *A lot.* We're the best of friends. But I'd like to be more. What I want to know is why you, Denver Jones, have a problem with me? Why do *you* think *I'm* not good enough for *your* sister, asshole?"

His eyes grow wide. He delicately shields his heart like I've caused incredible offense. "Are you accusing me of being a snob?"

I slam my hand on the table. "Answer the question."

"My objections have nothing to do with who you are. I don't want Darla near anyone with a penis. Darla will remain perpetually five years old in my mind. I mean, look at her!" He flails his arms to make his point.

"She doesn't look five years old, idiot." I'm dumbfounded.

"She's tiny. You're too tall for her. Find someone your own size." His scowl grows deeper.

"I'm not attracted to girls over six feet. It's a preference. We've had this conversation before. It feels like two wild stallions fighting to the death. Long arms, long legs, it's a mess. Besides, I'm crazy about Darla. Her height has nothing to do with it." I make my point and marvel at his ability to remain calm. Perhaps he's tuned me out, but he appears to be listening.

When I call the server to place my order, Denver stews and tries to construct a better argument. "Listen, it's not personal.

Darla's young and flaky. She doesn't know what she wants. It's like this photography bullshit. She's never going to do anything with it."

I glare without blinking. Denver loves his sister, but his engagement with her is minimal. He sees a toddler in a Chanel suit or a teenager playing house. It's no wonder he can't imagine her with a man---any man.

"Hey, dumbass, she's a working photographer." I reach into my back pocket, pull out my wallet, and dig through the leather flap. When I find Darla's glossy silver business card, I toss it across the table. "She's an excellent photographer. She did my firm's headshots, and our competitors loved them so much, she's booked through next year. Plus, she placed a bid with the city for the District Attorney's new website, but she knows that's a long shot. Give your sister a little credit. Your grandfather offered to make things easy for her. She wants to try it her way first."

He stares at the card and shrinks in his seat, ashamed for not giving her the benefit of the doubt. "Well, what about Brooklyn? Mom says she's already tired of it. She's thinking of selling her place."

I frown. "Darla loves her house. And she loves Brooklyn. We do the Farmer's Markets every Saturday morning and disco bowling every Sunday night. You know I wouldn't take your sister's money, right? If we got together, I'd sign a fucking prenup. I'm not a gigolo."

He nods and shudders. "You're making me sick, dipshit. I know you're a good person. I trust you more than any of the dicks my mother's lining up. If my sister must marry... and have sex." He swallows hard. "I suppose she'd be better off with someone like you. But don't push this! Take your time and let her come to you on her terms."

"That's fair. I really like her. You know I'd always take care of her."

He turns and watches the server set the plates on the table.

His voice grates as he inspects his favorite dish in Soho. "For fuck's sake, I'm not sure I can eat anymore. I was starving when I got here. You've ruined my appetite."

I cut my sandwich in half and grab the ketchup. "I might be mistaken, but did you clutch your pearls a moment ago?"

He chuckles. "You miss nothing. Do you? Hurry up, and eat. As soon as we're done, I'm heading to *Daniel's* to surprise bachelor number two with my fist."

DARLA

SAME TIME- MIDTOWN

"Hello. We're meeting Mrs. Davina Jones."

The young hostess nods and pivots to gaze at her monitor. Her forehead creases. "Davina Jones requested a reservation for three, and two people have arrived."

I smile. "Yes, but unless someone's manufactured a new design for a table that only seats three people, there should be an extra chair. My friend will join us." I gesture to Lana but keep my eyes on the dark-haired hostess who believes I'm too dumb for words.

She purses her lips and grabs another menu. "Of course. This way, please."

"Thank you for your flexibility." I chirp with a smile, straighten my posture, wiggle my shoulders, and follow her into the dining area. Lana buzzes behind me, dragging her feet every step of the way.

"Please stop yawning. It's rude." I whisper and skip a step, allowing her a chance to catch up.

"I don't know why I had to come. Demeter and I haven't spoken in weeks, and she's bound to demand an explanation. But

I'm done trying to explain my reasons, Darla. You hear me?" She yawns, then nearly trips over her feet as we round the corner into the main dining room. "I said done."

"Do you hear yourself? You're falling asleep because you spent the better half of the night---no, the better half of the week---getting sexed up by a man sixteen years your senior, and you dare to get high and mighty over Demeter marrying an older man. Love is love. Let it go." I peer over my shoulder and watch her mouth fall open.

Her breath explodes in a gasp. "Darla Jones, how dare you compare Liam and me to Angus and Demi. He's much older than her, and she's mining for gold. As a matchmaker and someone who believes in the importance of compatibility..."

"Oh, shut up. You're here because you owe me for weeks of forced wedding attendance. If you take up the fourth chair, they can't save it for bachelor number two. Now smile, they've spotted us." I shake my hair to give it that tousled, *devil may care* look and strut proudly on my new Mary Jane stilettos. The couture wrap-around dress is a personal favorite of Oscar's and gives me the confidence I desperately need in front of my snooty sister.

No one ever expects much from me. My parents didn't think I'd do much after graduation. I wasn't sure I would either. But now, I'm a professional woman, and responsibility agrees with me.

I run my own business and my own rules. And I don't care what anyone says. If I want to have dessert, then goddamn it, I'll have dessert.

My mother rises from her chair with her arms extended in a wide embrace. "Oh, my goodness! Darla! You look divine. Doesn't she look marvelous?" She turns to my sister, who offers nothing more than a shrug.

It doesn't matter. I'm not here to impress gold-digging tarts who marry men twice their age. I'm here for caviar and gossip.

Demeter's calm expression shifts dramatically when she spots

Lana skulking behind me. "Lana! Why haven't you returned my calls? I can't believe you've ghosted me all summer!"

I give my mother a kiss on the cheek and fold my body into the chair. Her shoulders stiffen when she realizes I've brought a guest and thwarted her plans. "Sweetheart, you should have told me you were bringing Lana. I would have asked for a larger table."

I unfold my napkin and lay it on my lap. My mother's comment makes no sense. Correction---it shouldn't make any sense. We're four people sitting at a table with four chairs. This is the perfect fit.

"Larger table? Don't be ridiculous. Four people, four sides, and four chairs. This is heaven sent." I exaggerate my giggle and lift my menu to shield my face. Behind my protective barrier, I listen to Lana lay on the judgment.

"You know how I feel about Angus, Demi. Of course, I'll attend the wedding. I swear I want to be supportive, but..." She takes a sip of water to wash away the sour taste in her mouth, and my sister pounces.

"But what? But what, Lana Howard? Are you too busy screwing Liam Fitzgerald?"

Lana shrieks.

Demeter hisses.

Adrenaline soars as accusations of hypocrisy and prostitution are flung with no consideration paid to the volume of their voices.

Accustomed to Demeter's outbursts, my mother orders a martini and asks the server to move us to a larger table. She offers no explanation, and I don't pry. Her plan is obvious.

Well, I've got plans, too.

This professional woman is not without resources.

"Sweetheart, Demi's wedding is two weeks away. Please tell me you've chosen your clothes for all three days. Remember,

Thursday night is casual---not too casual---but you know what I mean. Put everything on your father's card. We're going to have so much fun together." Mom starts slow, bringing up nonsense details as the first sip of gin from her dirty martini touches her lips.

I nod and lean close to the server. "I'll have a glass of Chardonnay, please."

I turn to my mother. "I'm almost done. The only dress not ready is the one for the church. I've got the final fitting next weekend. I'm wearing Aunt Daisy's rubies for the rehearsal dinner, and Nana's loaning me her cascading diamond and pearl necklace for the ceremony." The table grows silent.

Demeter whips her head so fast, strands of blond hair nearly strike my eyes. Her jaw drops. "Did she loan or give you that necklace? I could have worn it. *I am the bride.*"

My anger spikes. Demeter's never gone without, and yet she's perpetually preoccupied with what she doesn't have. I take a sip of wine and struggle to pass the liquid through my tightly clenched throat. "She's loaning it. She accompanied me to my fitting and offered them as the perfect accessory. Did you invite her to your fitting?"

"No, why would I?" Her voice drips with entitled outrage. She's such a jerk.

I wrinkle my nose and squint with derision. "Oh, I don't know. Because she's the only grandmother you have left, you love to ask her for money and you're having the reception at her estate... just for starters."

Nana Junie doesn't owe her a damn thing.

"You've got nerve. All you ever do is suck up to Nana and Papa. I've had enough of your bullshit, Darla!" She seethes through clenched teeth and shouts directly in my face. My lashes flutter from the wind of her breath. From the corner of my eye, I spot her claw-like hand flying towards my perfectly styled hair. There's no time to duck.

"Demeter! Don't you dare!" My mother intervenes in the nick of time.

"Your table's ready, ma'am." The server returns to move the unrefined, ill-mannered ladies making a scene to a larger table where more shenanigans are likely to ensue.

I can't believe I gave up a day in the park with Oscar for this.

"Why are we moving? Is someone else joining us?" Lana plays dumb while she scrolls through her messages. The wicked smile dancing on her lips tells me everything. Liam sent her a dirty text. Last week, she swore they were incompatible. One night of unbridled passion and the tide turned, but she still wasn't convinced. A few more times, and she's in love. She was already a know-it-all when it came to love and romance. Now, she'll be insufferable.

My mother playfully takes a seat and lies her ass off. "I just think it's nice to have lots of room in case we want appetizers and room to breathe." She takes a deep breath as if none of us know what breathing looks like.

As I slide into my chair, I look over my shoulder and make eye contact with an elderly couple seated across the room. They're dressed to the nines, sipping expensive whiskey, and look like they own the joint. I spotted them as soon as I walked in with Lana but kept that information to myself because I wasn't a hundred percent sure I'd need to call on their services. It was just a hunch. And as always, they were happy to oblige their favorite granddaughter.

I tap my temple and wink at Papa Desmond. He smirks, offers his hand to Nana Junie, and they move in for the kill.

"What a pleasant surprise! I thought I was spending the afternoon with the loveliest woman in Manhattan, and I run into four more." My grandfather's booming voice appears from behind a passing busboy and nearly knocks my mother out of her seat. "You don't mind if Juniper and I take these seats, do you?" He doesn't wait for a reply. When he pulls out Nana's chair, I rush around the table to greet them.

"What a surprise! They're not taken. We just wanted breathing room." I pat Lana's shoulder and point to my chair on the other end. "Take my chair, I want to sit next to my grandmother."

My mother growls with annoyance. "Damn it, Darla. Now we need a bigger table. Pierre Bishop's on his way."

Demeter giggles and chugs her wine in one gulp. Lana ignores her surroundings and amuses herself with Liam's texts.

Papa Desmond groans with displeasure. "Davina, Pierre Bishop is a cad."

Mom swirls the gin in her martini glass and purses her lips, irritated with his interference. "He comes from an excellent family. And no one says she needs to marry him. I'd just like her to have a date for her sister's wedding. A respectable date. A suitable one. Who knows what caliber of men she meets in Brooklyn? She spends so much time with that Oscar fellow."

"Caliber of men? *That Oscar fellow?*" The weight of her words makes my heart sink. A pout forms. I can't believe she'd say that out loud. He's Denver's best friend. I know he and I aren't an item, but who knows what might happen down the line? I've seen him stare. He's not made of stone. Eventually, I'll break through, and when I do, I'll latch on like the face-sucker in that *Alien* movie. By the time he catches on, I'll worm my way into his heart, and he'll never be free.

I'll admit that's not the best analogy, and it's terribly unromantic, but it was on two nights ago. When Oscar found out I'd never seen it, he made me stay up into the early hours to watch it.

I haven't been able to get it out of my mind.

Lost in thought, I can't hear the clamor of voices arguing around my head. Snaps of insults buzz between Nana Junie and my mother. Daddy isn't here to referee, and Mom has a long list of grievances dating back to my infancy.

Demeter chimes in about the pearl necklace, but Papa Desmond's raspy growl silences the table before she's able to submit a formal complaint.

"Please, stop talking about Darla's love life like she doesn't have any say in the matter. She's sitting right here." He turns a loving eye to me and smiles. "We know you're her mother, Davina. But Darla's a grown woman and a voting member of my Board of Directors. She knows her own mind."

Mother spills her martini on her dress. "Excuse me? Since when?"

Demeter shoots out of her chair. "Jesus Christ! It never ends!"

"Didn't I tell you?" I shift my eyes to my mother and shrink in my seat. My face heats under my sister's venomous glare. I know it's over the top, but I never realized it was a secret.

Oblivious to their shameless cronyism, my grandparents lean closer and offer to take me to one of our favorite pastimes, a Broadway show, that evening. Ever since I moved to Brooklyn, our nighttime outings have been few and far between.

"Can I take a rain check for later in the week? I've got a prior commitment." I lift my eyes to find my grandfather's suspicious smirk.

"What kind of commitment do you have on a Sunday night?" He teases and quirks a bushy brow. I've told him a dozen times manscaping is a real thing. He's worth billions, and appearances matter.

"Just stuff." I sit back in my seat, blink twice at Nana to hold her tongue, and reach for my glass of wine.

He slides it out of my reach. "I saw that blink."

"She bowls." Lana finally stops sexting Liam Fitzgerald long enough to forfeit her wingwoman duties and throw me under the bus. "She just started disco bowling on Sunday nights. Last week she scored a 200."

Oh, goddamn it. She said bowling.

"Bowling? Darla! You bowl! Is that what you do in Brooklyn?" Mom sways in her chair. "This is what I'm talking about. This is not who we are." She shudders with disgust and looks over her shoulder, fearing one of her society friends has overheard this gruesome revelation.

"Disco bowling?" Papa Desmond jumps to the edge of his seat. "Is that a thing? Darla Jones, how could you keep this from me?"

Goddamn it. She said disco.

Amid this chaos, Denver's friend and co-worker, Pierre Bishop, strolls by and skids to an awkward stop next to our table. His deep green eyes twinkle with amazement. We're all expecting him, but he pretends to be surprised to see us. *This is such a wild coincidence.* He leans into the table to say hello, but I'm not sure if the words ever fully make it out of his mouth.

A flash of denim and black cotton flies by before my mother screams bloody murder.

"Denver! No!"

EIGHT

OSCAR

LATER THAT EVENING-ODYSSEY LANES

"Long story short, after three scenes and one smackdown, the Jones Family are officially banned from *Daniel's Midtown*." Darla's cool blue eyes lock on mine, and her expression softens to a dreamy glow. I missed her all day. As soon as she told me she was ready, I raced down three flights of stairs and sprinted to her door.

"Remind me never to take you there." My eyes settle on the bridge of her nose, where I stop to count the freckles she's tried to disguise with concealer.

"I may not have to. They probably have a photo of our entire family with a note: *Please do not sell food to these people.*" She flutters her lashes playfully, and I make no move to look away. I relish this time to drink her in.

My gaze roams every swerve and kink of her petite frame, lingering on the swell of her breasts. I imagine what I'll touch first, how it might feel, how much of my hand will cover each supple mound, the color of her nipples, and the sweet taste of her pussy. How will she taste? How much longer do I have to wait?

A minute or more passes before she catches on.

"Are you okay? It's this shirt, isn't it? Do I look fat?" She pirouettes crudely on her bowling shoes and gifts me a bird's-eye view of her hot little ass in tight black leggings. My greedy hands instinctively reach out before I catch myself mid-air. I feel like I've lost my mind.

Darla's in play. Yeah, that's what's wrong with me. Things are different now. *Darla's in play.*

I've been silent too long. Darla's expecting something. A laugh, a chuckle, or a follow-up question about Pierre, but my heart is lodged in my throat, and words fail me.

"You didn't answer. Jesus Christ, I look fat. This shirt has to go." Darla stomps her foot and unties the knot she's fashioned at her waist to shorten the oversized shirt. "I don't remember voting for turquoise, anyway. Didn't we vote for red? We said red."

"Sorry, you don't look fat. Don't be ridiculous. And I like the knot. Keep it--- it's fucking adorable." I take a deep breath and let the cool air extinguish the fire raging inside me. When her cheeks spread and her mouth curves into a sweet smile, I feel the mojo I once had as a leather-clad teenager come back with a vengeance.

I can do this. I can win the cute girl. If I can make her smile, I can make her fall in love with me.

"And you're damn right we said red. It was four to one. Isn't that right, ANDY." Andrea Renaldi's swagger halts momentarily. A deep scowl forms. She knows she's in the wrong, but she won't let that interfere with this grievance.

"That's the worse one yet. If you're going to butcher it, be creative. And the place was out of red." She shrugs and tiptoes away in her matching turquoise capri pants.

"I don't believe you. You hate red and chose the short straw. We also didn't choose the name *Ball Breakers.* We decided on *Alley Cats.* If I recall, you're the only one who wanted *Ball Breakers.*

Were they out of that name too?" I shake the shirt in her face. "Are you truly so petty?"

She unzips her turquoise bowling bag, lifts a brand new, shiny turquoise glitter bowling ball, and carries it to our lane's ball return. "Oscar, you know I am. It's your fault for assigning me the job of ordering our gear. I've got red hair. Red doesn't go with red hair." Her nose crinkles.

Darla jumps to her feet and holds out her ponytail. "What's this?"

"That's auburn. It's not the same." She waves a dismissive hand and takes a seat in our lounge area.

"I have red hair." I point to my head.

"That's honey. This is red!" She holds out a strand of bright orange hair and curls it in her finger. "Curls trump waves. Mine is far less manageable than yours. And brighter. That hair goes with everything."

"If you're going to be a stickler. Harper's is a brighter shade of orange than yours. The entire team has orange hair. Cut your crap, Audrey." I grab her bowling ball and threaten to smear my fingerprints across the glossy exterior.

"Fine! I hate red, and I'd already ordered my ball. I won't charge anyone for the shirts." She kicks her legs, crosses them, then mumbles under her breath. "Bully jerk."

Darla slides across the slippery approach and bumps her hip into my leg. Her fingers twiddle with the knot on her shirt as she nervously shuffles her feet. "Hey, my grandparents are coming. I hope that's okay. I meant to tell you on the way here. Or maybe I should have asked. You know my Nana. Please, just call her Juniper. My grandfather, Desmond, loves disco. *It's his thing.* As soon as Lana mentioned this was disco bowling, he lost his shit. I couldn't say no."

"Disco? Seriously? The King of Park Avenue loves disco?" I stifle a grin as she nods and smiles from ear to ear. "Is that where you get your moves, little girl?"

She spins her forearms chest-level, then prances around me, practicing her footwork as she speaks. "Yes, sir. My grandparents taught me everything I know. In case it ever comes up in conversation or in one of your cases, they call this the *Proud Mary*."

I catch her arm and twirl her towards me. My gaze falls on her swollen lips, and my mouth waters to lick the seam, parting them until my tongue tangles with hers. When they curve into a slight smirk, I remember what I meant to ask. "Do you get anything from your Mom's side of the family?"

High-spirited voices answer for her. "Darla is *all Jones*."

My jaw hits the floor. Andrea jumps to her feet and emits a tiny squeak. Darla's grandparents arrive clad in a powder-blue leisure suit and a silver halter top disco dress, strutting and wiggling to the music. They look surprisingly good for their age, and their feet never stop.

Darla looks over her shoulder, unfazed by their attire, and offers each one a kiss on the cheek. "Did you have any trouble finding the place?"

"No, darling. Our driver grew up in the area. He found it fine. Introduce us, please." Desmond heads to Andrea with outstretched arms. She freezes.

"Andrea, these are my grandparents, Juniper and Desmond Jones. This is Andrea Renaldi, a Civil Rights attorney and a friend I met through Oscar. You've both met Oscar Brennan, Denver's best friend. He's my friend, too." Darla winks and draws lazy circles with her shoe. My heart grows wings.

"Nice to meet you." Unsure of what to do, Andrea curtsies then looks from side to side. After a quick handshake, she slinks back into her chair.

"Good to meet you. Darla speaks of you often." I give him a firm shake and let him size me up. He smiles and gives me a nod. Either he doesn't expect much from me, or he likes what he sees. I don't hold out hope for the latter.

"Call me Dez, and you can call her Junie. No formalities,

please. We're Darla's grandparents, not yours. Darla told us you have a full team. We're here for the music."

Darla laughs and playfully elbows her grandfather in the ribs. "This old man is far more fun than anyone believes. He used to make Nana leave my Dad with the babysitter for all hours of the night just so they could tear up Studio 54 with Liza and Halston." She shakes her head in mock judgment. "Utterly shameless."

Juniper blushes. "Only a few times. Dez loves to dance, and I can't say no to Dez."

As the players begin their first frames, Desmond surveys the room, then looks to me. "Aren't you missing players?"

Andrea lifts her wrist to check the time, then hops onto the seat of her chair. She glares towards the door before she scans the rest of the bowling alley, searching for the pair. "Harper and Edison went outside to talk. But that was twenty minutes ago."

Climbing down, she grabs her purse off the floor and whips out her phone. "I'll text her. They were arguing when they arrived. Maybe things escalated."

"Fighting over what?" I pull my phone from my back pocket and check if she's sent me a message. It's not like her to disappear without warning.

Andrea groans as her fingers stab violently into her screen. "Over what? What do you think? Two friends screw non-stop. They don't date anyone else. They act like they're married, but no one mentions commitment, no one admits they're in love, no one admits it isn't enough. But one day," she lifts her finger into the air to make a point, "it won't be enough, Oscar. Maybe that day is today." She shrugs and tosses her phone back in her bag. "But what do I know?"

"That's true. What do you know?" I tease.

She smiles, flips me off, and waves the finger slowly through the air while she sips her Margarita.

While we wait, the show must go on. I reset the player order and move Edison and Harper to the end of the line until we know more.

Darla snatches her child-sized ball from the return and dances the funky chicken for our enjoyment.

Yes, I know the funky chicken. I'm a son of Bay Ridge, Brooklyn, and if you're unfamiliar with this part of the world, those are the streets where John Travolta danced as Tony Manero in *Saturday Night Fever.*

I'm not just a great attorney. I've got untapped skills I previously assumed were useless.

But now I know better.

I used to lock myself in my room and watch decades' old reruns of Soul Train and Dance Fever, never knowing the girl of my dreams was somewhere across town learning the same steps with her grandparents.

This is strange and wonderful, and holy shit, I can't believe this deep dark secret might give me an advantage.

Darla makes her approach, and her blue eyes focus on the pins. She takes two steps forward, but that ends in a false start. She's not ready—not yet. Her posture steels for a second while she thinks.

She takes a deep breath, backs up, and adds a power step before she releases on a downswing. It sticks to the center. Her grandparents jump to the edge of their seats. She crouches, then leaps into the air when it strikes ten pins at once.

"And it's a STRIKE!" She throws her arms over her head and jogs in place. In customary fashion, disco balls drop from every lane, and the DJ spins the *Latin Hustle* in celebration.

"Did you see that?" She rushes to me with tears in her eyes. She's ecstatic. It's her first strike, and she feels like a kid who's just hit her first home run. I want to laugh, but I won't. Instead, I do what any real man would do in my situation.

I do the hustle.

I take four steps forward, clap, then four steps back and clap.

Darla's face lights up, and she quickly joins in. We turn four steps to the right, clap, then turn four steps to the left, and clap. And then we do the Travolta, but we can't finish because she curls her body into my chest and gets a case of the giggles.

"How could you keep this from me?" Her warmth catches me off guard. I've held her before, but now we have a chance. I don't have to pretend or hold back. I know I told Denver I wouldn't push it, but that doesn't mean I wouldn't tell her how I feel.

"All right, move off the approach. It's my turn." Andrea pushes us out of the way with her obnoxious glitter ball. "Harper and Edison bailed. Apparently, she's hired your friend Lana and Edison exploded in a fiery volcano of hot tears. Do your grandparents bowl, Darla?"

Desmond overhears and answers for her. "Hell, yes. I'll get our shoes!"

NINE

DARLA

LATER STILL-JUNIOR'S DINER

Oscar says the greasy spoon diner is a bowling tradition. We bowl, and then eat disgustingly fatty food that we have no right to consume since bowling doesn't burn this many calories. But a tradition is a tradition, and this one dates to the early 1990s when his Mom and Uncle Joe played on a team in Bay Ridge.

I don't question these things. I'm just here for the French fries.

Andrea taps her spoon on her strawberry shake to draw the table's attention. "As the person who came in second place..."

I interrupt her, "*Booooo!!* You beat Oscar by one point!"

"Hush up, losers!" She taps her spoon again. "I'd like to congratulate Dez Jones for the highest score, 235. That was fucking incredible. I say we throw Edison Reed out of the team." She uses her index and middle finger to whistle. I suspect she had too many Margaritas.

"Yay!!!! Grandpa!" I lift my root beer float in his honor. He laughs and clinks his cream soda with each one of our glasses. I haven't seen him have so much fun in years.

We all had fun. Oscar makes every day fun for me---he gets me.

For most of my life, only my grandparents understood me. Do you know how weird that is? You don't have to know. You can guess. It's as strange as it sounds. But he lets me be me and maybe even encourages it a little.

Tonight, he let himself be silly for me. In my world---north of 59th Street and east of Central Park---silly means undignified and trashy. But he didn't care. He embraced it and joined in.

When we danced, he stole the last piece of my heart. I'm on reserves now, and I'm afraid to go home without him. If I don't make him love me soon, I may wither and die.

Nana leans in and points to my buzzing phone. Her brow creases with concern. "Who keeps calling you?" She lifts her eye to the clock on the wall. It's almost midnight. "Who do you know that calls you at this hour?"

Oscar flips my phone over, and my mother's Siamese cat appears on the lock screen. "Your mom? Again? Maybe she's worried."

"I returned her text earlier. She knows I'm fine. That's not why she's calling." Things are going so well I don't want to mess them up with my mother's expectations and demands. Between Denver's psychosis and Demeter's society wedding---something Oscar loathes---I don't want to come off as the needy girl.

The needy girl needs things---like dates to her sister's wedding.

I want to be the cool girl. Those are the girls boys fall in love with. I think I read that somewhere---or saw it on a show.

"Andrea, Oscar, I read about your Supreme Court case, and I don't need to tell you I am dying of envy. That's a lawyer's dream." Papa wags a fry while he speaks.

Oscar's face turns red, and my heart bursts with pride for the man I love. "Thank you, sir. You're right. It was a dream and Andrea's case. She let Harper and I tag along."

Their words move Andrea to tears. She's definitely drunk. "Oscar was indispensable. He's the best litigator." She sniffles and wipes her nose with her napkin.

I squeeze Oscar's forearm and cringe when my phone buzzes again. Seconds later, Nana lifts her phone and shows me a horribly unflattering photo of my mother. The name Davina appears on top. It's her caller ID photo. Nana's cattier than I gave her credit.

Her eyes bug. "How does she know I'm with you? She can only suspect. It's way past my bedtime. Sweetheart, what on earth does she want?"

My shoulders sag as I slurp the rest of my root beer float. "She's coming over at dawn to drag me home for a makeover. She wants me to meet a bevy of bachelors closer to my age, unfamiliar to Denver. Despite my protests, I've got appointments lined up through tomorrow evening, all in the hopes of finding me a date for Demeter's wedding."

Papa Desmond's ears perk. He leans into Nana with ketchup-stained lips and points to Oscar. "Darling, this is an easy fix. Tell your mother you've got a date. Tell her you're taking Oscar. Do you have plans two weekends from now?"

Oscar shakes his head. "No, I don't." He turns to me. His steel-blue eyes smolder with a fiery lust I might only be imagining since my grandparents are less than two feet away. "Do you want me to be your date? You know I will if you do." My pulse skitters. He brushes a loose strand of hair off my cheek, and my mind swirls with images of Mr. Darcy.

He chuckles. "Sorry, you had some cheese on your face."

"I was saving that for later." Okay, not Mr. Darcy.

"Are you sure you want to go? You hate stuff like that. It's three days of putting up with Demeter's ilk and the New York Social Register." I give him an out but wet my lips to make it difficult.

His eyes search mine, and the intensity of his gaze makes me regret my words. I can't go with anyone else. Now that Oscar's on the table, no one else will do. "I'm sure, Darla." His pupils expand, and his mouth twitches into a smile. "I'd do anything for you."

"You would?" My heart thunders and throbs in my ears.

Nana interrupts our flirtations to offer extra insurance against my mother's shenanigans and install herself in the wingwoman hall of fame. "Better yet, why don't you tell your mother Oscar's your boyfriend. She can switch your date, but she can't switch out your man. When she arrives tomorrow morning, have Oscar answer the door without a shirt and bed hair."

"Nana!" I feign offense for Oscar's sake, then shift my eyes to gauge his reaction.

"Sounds fine to me. I have no problem being your boyfriend and hamming it up in front of your folks. I'll play the part perfectly. Just let me grab clothes on the way home." Words fly out like bullets from a machine gun hitting me left and right.

I stare dumbfounded and try to process his words. Fake boyfriend? *What about a real one?*

He reads my expression and leans closer. "Hey, are you okay with me sleeping at your place?"

Nana jumps in and answers for me. "She's got five bedrooms. She has room. Oh, my God! Can you picture the look on your mother's face? I'd love to be a fly on the wall! You better call me when she leaves."

TEN

OSCAR

A WEEK LATER- FALLON, RENALDI & BRENNAN-SOHO

"Hey, dumbass, I'm starving. Let's go eat." Edison Reed, Executive District Attorney for New York County, pops his head into my office and shocks me out of my lovesick daze. I don't have time for this.

I lift my eyes to the door but keep my head down, focused on editing my closing statement. Two more sentences, and I'm done. "I've got no time for you, idiot. I'm having lunch with Darla. She's swinging by in fifteen minutes. Go bother Harper. I'll bet that's why you're really here. Right?"

I glance at my watch, then return to my statement. "Now it's thirteen minutes. Go away!"

He ignores my instructions and barges in, uninvited. I know what he's doing. He wants to get under my skin before tomorrow. I'm about to wipe the floor with his pretty-boy face, and he hates to lose. "Why must you waste the jury's precious time? I offered a plea bargain, and tomorrow it goes away. Your client is guilty---*I know it, and you know it.* And if my intel is correct, all twelve jurors know it too."

I scoff and continue to type. "My client is innocent. I've got the same intel, and it overwhelmingly favors me. Mark my words, when I finish exonerating her, I'm going to help her sue your arrogant detectives and the NYPD for racial profiling. Your evidence was entirely circumstantial and, frankly, ludicrous. Drop the charges before I hand you your ass on a silver platter."

I smirk and raise my middle finger over my monitor. "Suck this, Eddie. Suck it hard."

"Don't call me Eddie. I finally got my mother to stop calling me Eddie. If she can do it, so can you." He flips me off, then struts confidently towards my desk. We've known each other since junior high, and although we work as adversaries, we don't let our jobs come between us---most of the time.

Happy with my edits, I hit print and rush to the printer to grab my statement. Darla promised to give it the once over during lunch, and she hates reading off my phone. She's the perfect copy editor. She's got eyes like an eagle, and she loves correcting my grammar.

Just this once, I'll make use of her annoying habit.

I swipe the papers off the tray and hold them against my chest, away from Edison's prying eyes. He leans in and squints, optimistic that this will be the day his x-ray vision kicks in.

I nudge him out of my path, toss my statement into a folder and glide it into my bag. A quick glance to the clock on my computer tells me I've got five minutes before Darla sashays her tight little ass through my door.

God, I love that cute ass.

She's my favorite part of the day, and I haven't seen her since yesterday afternoon. Between her sister's wedding and this case, we've had to synchronize our watches and calendars to plan random outings, coffee breaks, or lunches.

If I had more time, we wouldn't be where we are now. We wouldn't be dancing around a fake bullshit relationship for the sake of her sister's wedding.

We'd be together. *Engaged.* Is it too soon for that?

I hope that's what she wants. I know I do. Most days, it feels like we're already married.

After the initial shock of finding me half-dressed at Darla's house, Mrs. Jones accused us of faking this fake relationship. That didn't go over well. Outraged by her mother's suspicions, Darla refused to give her the satisfaction of coming clean.

Now she suspects we're being followed. So we're all in. Whenever we're together in public, we're together. *A couple in love.*

It feels as natural as breathing, except for the kissing part. We should be kissing. A couple in love should be kissing. *Kissing day and night—night and day.*

But I can't kiss her if we're only pretending. I need to kiss her when it's for real. Because when I kiss her, I won't be able to stop. Maybe never.

Goddamn, I want to kiss her so badly, I can hardly think of anything else. Which isn't good since I'm currently fighting for my client's freedom.

Concentrate, fucker.

"Jesus Christ, Oscar. Answer me. Did you see who Harper left with?" Ed slaps the side of my head to bring me back to the land of the living. I jerk forward and instinctively punch his gut.

Ed needs to go. Now.

"You were leaving?" I reach for my jacket and gesture towards the door. There's no sense in dropping hints. He's clueless to social cues.

"I am?" He looks behind him.

"Yes, Darla's coming. I want to head out as soon as she gets here." I gesture again, more emphatically this time, flailing my arm towards the open door.

"Darla, huh? Did something happen recently?" He offers a wolfish grin.

"None of your business."

"Does Denver know you're banging his baby sister?" He folds his arms at his chest and feigns concern.

I gnash my teeth and groan, "I never want to hear you use the word *banging* regarding Darla. Have some fucking respect."

He lifts his hands and mocks surrender. "I didn't mean to disrespect your woman, but it's about time you close that deal. You spend almost every waking hour with this girl. The least you can do is satisfy her needs. Or your own, if you still have them."

"When I want to be with Darla, I'll be with Darla. I won't take female advice from someone like you." My heart clenches tightly in my chest.

Of course, I want to be with her. I want to be with her as soon as she walks through that door.

Damn, am I taking her for granted? I'm not entirely sure how she feels. We're not sleeping together. If we were, I wouldn't want to stay friends. I won't be like Edison and Harper. Screw benefits---I want the whole enchilada. Rings. A honeymoon at Niagara Falls. Babies with her eyes and my even temper.

I swallow hard and continue. "If it happens, we'll be together legitimately. No bullshit. No games or denial about what things are or might become. The last thing I need in my life is a friend with benefits. I don't want *a Harper*."

I lift my wrist to show him the time and tap my watch. "Hey, you need to go. I don't want you here when Darla arrives. You annoy her."

At the mention of Harper, he stops pacing and snaps his head in my direction. "What the fuck does that mean? What the shit's wrong with Harper? She runs circles around Darla..."

I throw a pen at his head and cut him off. "Watch your mouth, Darla's fucking stunning. And nothing's wrong with Harper, dipshit. She's beautiful and smarter than both of us put together. Plus, she's incredibly patient to put up with your dumb ass. I said I don't want *a Harper*. I don't want to have sex with a woman I'm in love with, then turn around and pretend we're just friends. You know you're in love with Harper---right? You can't be that dense." My words come out like a hard slap, but as always, he shakes them off and refuses to let them sink in.

He shrugs dismissively. "We love each other, but we're not in love. I've been in love before, Oscar. That sucked---this doesn't. Harper and I are best friends. Not everyone needs a commitment to have a good time."

"You're an idiot. But I'm glad you don't love her. This is the third day this week she's eaten lunch out of the office." I grab my keys and slide them into my pocket.

"Who's an idiot? Oh, you..." Darla suddenly appears at my threshold, and my pulse jumps at the sight. Her new cashmere sweater, the one I helped her pick out, hugs each breast so perfectly, my cock tremors to life. Her long auburn hair sweeps past her face and cascades off her delicate shoulders.

I love it when she wears her hair down. I want to see it fall off a pillow when she's lying next to me at home in bed...and I'm ramming my fucking cock so hard she needs to hold on to the nightstand for fear she'll fly off the mattress.

What? What happened? I wipe the sweat off my brow and refocus.

"Are you ready?" She asks me, but she narrows her gaze at the idiot standing in the middle of my office. Her shoulders tense with discomfort. Her swollen lips purse before she lets out a huff and blows those adorable bangs off her face. Ever since Harper made a choice to shake Ed loose, Darla and Andrea observe a strict girl code. They give no common courtesy.

Without acknowledging or greeting Ed, she turns to me, "Do you want me to wait by the elevators?"

One bat of those thick eyelashes, and my heart stumbles into my sternum. Hazy with unrequited lust, I search my mind then swipe my bag off the floor. "No, Eddie's leaving."

ELEVEN

OSCAR
ROBERTA'S CAFÉ- SOHO

"I'M SORRY IF I EMBARRASSED YOU. I SHOULDN'T BE SO CURT with your friend." Darla talks as she reads. Her wide eyes peer over the stack of papers in her hands, then flutter back to the boring text I've forced her to proof. I don't know what she's talking about---she could never embarrass me.

I take a gulp of cold beer and set my glass down on the wobbly table. Annoyed with the imbalance, I grab two sweetener packets and shove them beneath the shorter table leg. When it doesn't do the trick, I insert one more.

Presto! We're in business.

Darla smiles, impressed with my ingenuity, and gives it a test of her own. When it remains steady, she offers me a playful salute.

I wish she'd let me take her somewhere nicer than *Roberta's*. There's no denying the food's great, but sometimes I think she deliberately slums it to keep me from spending too much on her.

I know I don't have her kind of money, but I can afford better than this dive. Her couture clothes seem out of place. Her

Hermès bag, which she insists is a hand-me-down from her grandmother, is the envy of every woman here. If you throw in her diamond stud earrings and the Rolex watch, she's wearing more than I make in a year.

The only thing I'm embarrassed about is my inability to give her the life she's accustomed to. She shouldn't compromise for me. What if I'm naïve?

"I see you staring at my watch. I'm dressed this way because I'm meeting my mother this afternoon. I don't want her to think you've asked me to tone it down because we see each other. She has that stereotype about men who don't come from money. That they'll hold it against me. I know we're not really seeing each other, but do you think it's true? Would you hold it against me?" I stare, bewildered, fascinated by her lips. Heart-shaped and stained with a frosted pink gloss, I bet they taste like strawberries.

"Never. You are who you are. Does it bother you to be with someone with less?" I lower my voice and pull my eyebrows together. I've always assumed I know the answer, but maybe I don't. While I wait for her reply, I brace myself for the possibility that she may have concerns.

She lowers my closing statement and sets it neatly on the table. Her eyes search the room like the right words have gone missing. They're lost somewhere between the kitchen and the front door. She shifts her gaze to me and sighs with remorse. "I thought you knew me better than that. I'm not my sister."

My chest expands to make room for my exploding heart. "No, you're not. You're Darla Jones. There's no one like Darla Jones."

An impish smile spreads across her face and reaches her bright eyes. "I was hoping you'd notice."

My heart labors under the weight of her gaze. I think I'll kiss her today. Today feels right.

She sinks her teeth into her bottom lip and extends her arm

to reach for her glass of water. Before she takes a sip, a loud ping rattles her. She dips her hand into her purse, pulls out her phone, and cringes.

"Sorry, it's my Mom. Demeter's wedding is four days away, and new problems arise daily. Did I tell you my sister doesn't want to sign the pre-nuptial agreement? My parents' lawyer says Angus has three daughters, not two. Demeter's unhappy with that split and wants to head back to the table. Things may go down to the wire." She shudders with disgust.

"Darla Jones! There you are!" A familiar voice appears from the far side of the café.

In an unprecedented move, Darla hops into my lap and wraps her arms around my neck. "For the love of God, follow my lead."

She smashes her cleavage into my chest, kisses my cheek, and giggles flirtatiously into my ear. When her mother draws closer, she feigns surprise. "Mom! For heaven's sake, what are you doing here? Oscar has such a quick lunch, and every minute counts."

With her eyes adrift, mine linger on the two mounds of supple flesh lurking just beneath her modest neckline. I've recently concluded my hands might be a perfect fit. Hand size is proportional to height. She's lucky I'm as tall as I am, or there would be definite spillage.

"Will you please stop ogling my daughter in front of me?" Her mother catches me in the act and tries to shame me. I'm too lovesick to care. She should see what's lurking underneath, trying to bust out of my trousers.

"Leave him alone. We're in love. There's nothing here he hasn't seen." Darla straightens her shoulders and slinks back to her chair. "Please state your business. My man is due back at work soon."

"Sweetheart, Demeter had plans to tell you herself, but I was afraid she'd say something hateful and hurt your feelings. Please

understand this is not coming from me. This is from your sister."
She wrings her hands and avoids eye contact with her daughter.

"Is she uninviting me?" Darla snaps.

"No, she can't do that. But it's her wedding, and she doesn't want you to bring Oscar. She's afraid you'll misbehave and take attention away from her. If you and Oscar are a legitimate couple, I understand if you don't want to attend without him. I wouldn't want to go if someone didn't want the man I love." She pats Darla's trembling hand and wipes a non-existent tear.

"I see." Darla's icy tone unsettles me. She narrows her gaze, but with her ginormous eyes, it's hardly noticeable. "Oscar, we'll grab lunch on the way back to your office."

I lift her bags and help her out of her chair. "Whatever you want."

She gives my hand a light squeeze but maintains her composure.

"Sweetheart, please say something." Mrs. Jones blocks our retreat, but we move past her then make a hard stop.

"Tell your daughter she has four days to find another venue for the reception. Please remind her our grandfather signed the estate in Rye over to me on my twentieth birthday. I'll ask the groundskeeper to tear down her tents tonight." She slides her extra-large sunglasses onto the bridge of her nose to mask the dark flush overtaking her cheeks.

"Darla!"

We walk in silence and hold hands until we reach the safety of my office.

Darla doesn't have to say she's sorry because she did nothing wrong. But she needs me to hear it. She needs me to know she doesn't feel the way her mother and sister do.

"Oscar, you're the best person I know." Tears flood the bluest eyes I've ever seen, and my heart clamors to kiss each drop away.

I need to end this torture now---for both of us.
But my girl deserves more than just a happy ending.
I won't let this ugly day be the way we begin.

TWELVE

DARLA

THE FOLLOWING EVENING- BROOKLYN

"Breathe, Darla. I haven't heard you inhale since we passed City Hall." Lana wiggles my shoulder and leans in to listen for the sound of my breath. The scent of her perfume triggers my allergies, and strands of hair tickle my nose. With her enormous head in my way, I can't cover my mouth, and I accidentally sneeze on her cheek.

"Oh my God, I'm so sorry." I cover my face in horror, then reach for my purse to make amends. "I've got some tissue and hand wipes to dab the residue. Don't dab too hard, or you'll wipe off your makeup." I snatch a tissue for myself and avert my eyes. I've lost all sense of decorum.

"No, it's fine. You're in pain." She mops up my mess and returns to her side of the limo, opposite me.

I didn't throw my sister off my property. Perhaps if it wasn't four days leading up to her wedding, I might have considered it. But if she wants to be a jerk on her big day, so be it. She's been a jerk her entire life. Why stop now?

I won't let her make me ruthless and cruel---that's not who I am.

She can kiss my ass if she thinks she'll ever have access again. But I'll be the bigger woman and let her have it for her precious wedding weekend.

I won't be attending and was happy with my regrets. I expected as much until it started the chain reaction from hell.

I look for the East River and listen for the changing pitch of the tires when we cross onto the bridge. I feel better already. With every passing week, Brooklyn feels more like home.

"I'm not sorry I declined. She did a terrible thing." Lana mumbles as she smooths on a fresh coat of lip gloss. She rubs her lips together and smacks them repeatedly before she continues. "Serves her right."

"You never wanted to go in the first place." I roll my eyes and shoot a sarcastic grin at Harper, texting furiously on the other side of the car.

Andrea fusses with her hair and nods. "Well, I wanted to go. Someone better get married soon. I finally find an evening gown that hugs my figure perfectly without making me look like a hoochie mama, and we stage a political boycott. It's so unfair." She clicks the bottom of her heels on Harper's knees. "Please stop texting Ed. Have some pride, woman."

Harper jumps at the mention of Ed's name. She shifts uncomfortably in her seat, then tucks her phone in her purse. Her hands tremble, but she shoves them in her pockets to keep us from calling her out. "What? I'm not texting him."

"Are you okay?" I check in but keep my question vague.

She nods and offers a smile that never reaches her eyes.

"I don't know why we're meeting her. She'll be rude and demanding. She'll throw an epic tantrum and blame you for ruining her wedding. This is a waste of time." Lana scrolls through her phone then stares wistfully into space, using her fingers to count something off. When we hit a bump in the road, she's sure she's lost count and starts over.

"How many people canceled?" Andrea stares out the window,

always fascinated by Brooklyn, as if it's so different from Lower Manhattan. We've crossed a portal into a different world.

"Last count, eighty-four. First, me and Oscar. Lana and Liam jumped on the bandwagon. Denver told Demeter to go to hell. His law school buddies canceled. They were only flying to see him and Oscar. Nana and Papa Desmond had a conniption. They bailed and did it in such a grandiose manner, their friends followed. Things got ugly fast." I shake my head and try not to laugh. It's not funny. Not really.

"How many guests are left?" Harper's weak voice breaks through.

"I don't think she invited more than a hundred and twenty. She wanted something exclusive."

"And she got it... damn it, I lost count again." Lana clenches her fist with rage and pulls out her planner.

The limousine cruises into the parking lot of Junior's Diner, the greasy spoon we frequent every Sunday night after bowling. Demeter asked to meet at our parent's house, but I won't be blindsided. If she wants to meet, she'll need to step out of her element.

If she makes demands, I walk.

"Do you think she'll show?" Andrea steps out of the car and waits for Harper.

"I've reserved the Barry Manilow party room for privacy, and she's agreed to meet us here promptly at 6:00pm. If she doesn't show, it's no skin off my back. I'm hungry." I stand by while Lana packs her huge planner and shimmies her long thighs out of the car.

"Can we stop at a pharmacy on the way home?" She forces a smile and hugs her chest, rubbing her arms to create friction.

"I sneezed on you ten minutes ago. I couldn't have made you sick so fast." I hold the back of my hand to her forehead and feel beads of cold sweat. "Do you want to wait in the car?"

"No, ma'am. Let's nail this..."

"I do!" Harper screams from the other side of the limo. "I'll wait here. My presence will only throw off your game. Come get me when she leaves." She never explains or waits for us to respond. She flies into the car and slams the door.

"What the hell?" I turn to face Andrea's shocked expression.

"I'll explain inside. Consider me your attorney. I'm excellent, Darla." She takes a notepad and pen from her purse and scribbles.

"Do you know I argued a case in front of the Supreme Court?" She taps her pen on her pad and writes the number one.

My eyes grow wide. "Jesus Christ, Andrea. I don't have time for your resume. We've got five minutes. Let's do this."

THIRTEEN

OSCAR

THE NEXT MORNING-SOHO

YESTERDAY WAS A GOOD DAY. AFTER A YEAR OF BAD PRESS, AND time away from her children, my client is fully exonerated and free to grieve the loss of her husband. She'll never entirely recover, and my heart goes out to her children.

I just wish I could do more.

Darla set up an anonymous college fund for her daughters behind my back. I'm not supposed to know, and I won't rat Andrea out, but I have far too many clients in need. That can't become a regular thing. I learned a long time ago, it's better to change the system than simply throw money at it.

But I love her heart. I love every little inch of Darla Juniper Jones.

My case is done. My client is free. *No more fucking excuses.*

I gather my files into a tall stack, lift, tap to straighten, then transfer them into a box. Every note, memo, scribbled legal pad gets marked and piled neatly into a box for future reference. You can never be too careful. Once my client is exonerated, she can't be tried again, but you never know when evidence from one case might come in handy for another. I swear I'm not a packrat, but my notes are sacred.

"Oh my God, did Darla brief you?" Andrea tears open the door. We're closed today and tomorrow. Everyone is off for dumb Demeter's wedding weekend, but it's so last minute we're scrambling to shutter the office.

"What do you think?" I point to my jeans. "Do I look like I'm working today?"

She lifts her palms, wiggles her head, and sticks out her tongue. "All right. So sorry, Mr. Brennan." She glides her behind onto my desk and helps me tape my box. "We had so much fun last night."

"I heard. Darla says you made Demeter cry." I carry my box into the closet and place it on top of the others. I need more storage.

She jumps off my desk, unplugs my laptop, and winds the cord through the power adapter. "She's a cry-baby. You don't come to the table with nothing to offer and make demands. Darla held all the cards. It was a lawyer's dream, Oscar!" She hands me the cord, and I follow her into the hall.

"So, what did you ask? Darla fell asleep before she told me the rest of the story." I stuff my laptop into my bag and check my phone for Desmond's message. He's taking me shopping. I can't believe I agreed, but he's incredibly persuasive. And I want to look suitable for Darla. If we love each other as we are, there's no harm in adding a little window dressing.

Andrea flings her purse over her shoulders, then uses her fingers to illustrate. "Number one— tonight's caviar and cocktail bullshit is now a barbecue by the lake. That one is mine. You know how much I love barbecue. Dez is flying in some guy from Buffalo. I'm so excited." She jumps for joy.

I stare, confused. "I thought these were Darla's demands."

"Oh, shut your mouth. She said this was a group effort. Number two— you get a disco hour at the reception. That's mainly for Dez, but she thought you'd have fun with it as well. Number three— no cutting you out of family photos. And four— Angus makes a sizable donation to the Brooklyn Humane Society---we passed a flyer on the way in. I told her she could get more, but Demeter's crocodile tears moved her." She zips her computer bag and checks her watch.

"I really like Darla." Her amber eyes peek through her disheveled curls.

"I do, too. I'm going to tell Darla tonight. No matter what." I stare through the glass doors and into the street. "She's the one--- I wish I'd told her from the start."

I spot a black car signal right and head towards our side of the street. It must be Desmond. "Hey, Andrea..."

A jarring noise makes me turn. Andrea slams her desk drawer and points a finger in my direction. "You better not hurt her, Oscar. She loves you. Love doesn't come around every day. It's a miracle meant to be cherished and nurtured. You treat her right, for fuck's sake."

"What about Judge Fratini? He's nuts about you, and you keep kicking him to the curb? Why isn't his love cherished and nurtured?" I draw a heart in the air, then make a breaking gesture with my hands.

"All right. Get out. I'll see you tonight."

FOURTEEN

DARLA

THE SAME DAY- FIFTH AVENUE

"HEAR ME OUT. I'VE PUT HOURS INTO THIS." LANA MUMBLES AND flips through her obnoxiously overstuffed planner. Her fingers walk across the pale pink paper, dancing through rows of contacts and pulling out business cards from secret pockets. When she finds what she's looking for, she stomps her stilettos and chirps with joy.

"Found it! This lady is a goddess. Let her work her magic on you. You will not be sorry." Her eyes twinkle with excitement.

"Magic. Please, no magic. I know what magic means. Magic means too much makeup, a corset, and my big tits spilling out in front of my childhood priest. I can't bear it." I feel the hot bile rise from my roiling stomach.

"Nonsense. You already know Oscar likes your personality. He leers at your behind like it's a slice of prime rib cooked in butter. I've seen it for myself. He shamelessly salivates." She dabs powder on her nose, then quickly tucks her compact away when the car slows. While I gather my bags, Lana throws her planner into her purse and swings the door wide open.

"He does?" I haven't seen any saliva. Why does he hide it from me?

"Yes, ma'am. I caught him red-handed last weekend when you bent over the stove to pull out your snickerdoodles."

I'm speechless. "Are you sure he wasn't just eyeing the cookies? Oscar loves sweets."

"Stop being so modest. Oscar was eyeing *your* cookies." She giggles and pumps her fists in the air. "So, stop covering up the goods, dummy. Let him see what Darla Jones has to offer. Maybe he'll finally get off his ass and gobble you up. This weekend is the perfect opportunity to reel that man in. He's already yours. Let him know you feel the same."

I skitter to the end of the sidewalk and keep my head down as I meander through the crowd of commuters. I can't breathe. Lana's plans have bumped my anxiety from a solid eight to an eleven in a matter of seconds.

My heart can't take this kind of pressure. When the crowd moves into the crosswalk, I bolt onto the street, desperate to breathe the fresh air of the park. But all I get is a mouth full of exhaust.

"Stop staring at me like I'm crazy." Lana takes my hand and drags me up towards Fifth Avenue, barreling through people like a bowling ball tearing through pins. I'm mortified by her aggression, and I apologize each step of the way.

"What's gotten into you? Last night, you were sick. Now, you've got the energy of a wolverine." I know that look---the bubbly enthusiasm. I've seen it a hundred times.

"I'm a professional. It's about time you learn why people pay so much for my services. You've spent years hot and bothered over that strange man. I don't know what you see in him, but I see the way your face lights up whenever he's nearby. He's your match. You found him. You staked him out, then made him fall head over heels in love. Now I'm going to help you close this deal." Lana points to a tawdry lingerie boutique and emits a sound resembling a hissing cat. "Let's get him, tiger."

"What the hell was that?" I quirk an eyebrow.

"That was my tiger. Come on, this lady is gold." She digs her hands into my shoulders and pushes me through the decorative doors.

"Why do I feel I'm heading into a crazy Cinderella makeover? I'm not one of your clients. Don't go overboard." I warn her as a French woman pulls me into a dressing room. I sense regrets are just around the corner.

There's no denying she's effective, but all that success comes from relentless dedication to her job. This is her chance to prove herself, and she won't give up easily. In order to make my dreams come true, she'll pull out all the stops.

But what choice do I have? I'm hanging on hope, a wing, and a prayer.

This weekend could be my last chance. Oscar's dawdling defies explanation. I think he likes me. He acts like he wants me. Every time I think he's going to shower me with kisses and carry me upstairs, he backs away and leaves me hanging.

It's not fair. *Where the hell are my kisses?*

"Where the hell are my kisses, Lana!"

"Just around the corner. I promise." She answers from behind the curtain.

We've had four months of friendship. The good kind. We hang out almost every day and talk into the small hours of the night.

Oscar's a perfect gentleman. *Too perfect.*

There's been no accidental manhandling.

No alcohol-fueled close calls.

He's copped no feels. It's infuriating.

I'm twenty-two years old and head over heels in love. Oscar is more than a gorgeous face and hot body--he's got a big heart and a warm soul. He's perfect.

And goddamn it, I'm so horny.

"Dear Lord, am I Harper? Is that who I've become, Lana? *Am I Harper?* Please don't tell me I'm Harper Fallon. I can't bear the thought of chasing a man for years with no end in sight." I wrestle myself out of the third bustier forced on me in fifteen minutes and chuck it over the dressing room curtain.

Before it hits the floor, I'm slammed by a wave of hushes. Lana throws herself against the thick drape and shoves her pinched face through the crack. Her angry green eyes find mine, and hateful words tumble out before I shield my naked breasts from her view.

"Good Lord, Darla. Lower your damn voice. Harper is on her way here. If you weren't so self-absorbed, you would have heard me mention she hired me a week ago." She peers over her shoulder then hands the saleslady my discarded piece.

"Harper? Coming here?" I struggle to hold my breasts in my hands, aware one tiny shift or miscalculation will result in Lana getting a close-up of my nipples. "Do you mind?" I gesture for her to retreat.

She turns to leave, then circles back. Her eyes roam too freely for my comfort. "Darla..."

"What?"

"You've got some pretty spectacular tits. Let's get you a plunging neckline sundress for the barbecue. Mark my words that virginity is toast." She turns to the saleslady and calls for champagne.

FIFTEEN

OSCAR

LATE AFTERNOON- BROOKLYN

My phone pings for the second time in five minutes. I know it's Darla, and she has every right to nag.

We should have left fifteen minutes ago. I toss a few more items into my luggage, zip up my toiletry kit, and place my suit bags by the door.

Desmond got carried away. A quick excursion to shop for one suit became a three-hour expedition to the finest couture stores on Fifth Avenue. Commission-hungry salesmen vied for my attention by tossing silk ties, French cuff dress shirts, wool slacks, and Italian leather shoes at me left and right. I felt like Julia Roberts in *Pretty Woman*. I'll never wear half of what he bought.

Before he brought me home, I told Desmond how I feel about Darla. I spared him details because I should bare my soul to her first. But in a roundabout way, I wanted to ask for his blessing. He gave me a pat on the back and wished me luck.

I may never have her parent's approval, and we'll have to live with that. I'm not naïve. I know we come from different worlds. Her grandparents mean the world to her. If they believe in us, we'll start with someone on our team.

I swipe my phone from my dresser and text Darla I'm on my way. I can't wait to see her. Something is simmering in the air, and the longer the day grows, the more my skin prickles with anticipation.

Four months of madness have brought us to today. I could be wrong, but I think Darla feels it too. *Two texts to tell me I'm ten minutes late?* She can't be that eager to get to Rye.

I sling my bags over my shoulders, lock my door, and race to the sidewalk. Desmond showed me photos of the estate in Rye--- it's set on two acres overlooking Long Island Sound. Darla and I can sneak away from everyone and walk the grounds by the water. We can set up tiki lamps or sit on the wraparound porch. He said her room has a balcony facing the beach and a fireplace if it gets chilly.

Rye is the perfect place to tell her how I feel. And who knows, it might lead to something more.

I won't push this. After four months of dragging my feet, there's no sense in rushing things now. If Darla lets me kiss her--- we'll kiss. I'm not an animal. I can approach her with delicate hands and woo her like the gentleman I believe I've proven myself to be.

Halfway up her stoop, with my eyes cast down, I hear Darla's French doors swing open. "I know I'm late, and I see your car parked out front. We'll get going just as... soon..." Lust clouds my vision. "As we get our..." I swallow hard, too enthralled by my first unrestricted view of Darla's naked cleavage. Where did this dress come from? Dainty white flowers on thin blue fabric surround a plunging neckline and leave nothing to my imagination. It's so thin, I can nearly see the shape of her nipples.

"Is something wrong?" She steps closer. The faint jiggle of her supple flesh is almost imperceptible, but I see it. My cock swells and throbs against my thigh. Every hair stands on end.

"Darla..." My voice trembles. I shake my head to clear my lust-addled brain and settle my gaze on hers.

Our eyes lock, and she takes another step, closing the distance between us. "You were saying?"

I tilt my head and lean closer. For a moment, I close my eyes and breathe her in. "Grapefruit, lilac, and Darla sweat. They could sell that scent at Saks."

Her eyes flare wide. "I forgot about that. Do you like me, Oscar? Please say you do, or I wore this crazy dress for nothing."

I shake my head, nod, then shake my head again. "Darla. Darla Juniper Jones, how can you not see that I am madly in love with you? But yes, I like you, too. You're my favorite person in the entire world."

She draws a quick breath, then lifts her eyes to mine. Her bottom lip quivers, but she holds it steady with her teeth. "What took you so long?"

The truth hurts too much to say out loud, but she deserves to hear it. She had every right to move on. But she didn't.

Darla's a catch. Loads of wealthy pricks are combing their hair, trimming their pubes, and spraying cologne on their dicks, hoping to steal her away at the barbecue. Jesus Christ, the thought infuriates me. I hope they get a rash.

I trail a finger down her forehead and let it fall into the thick streams of her auburn hair. A soft whimper escapes her pink lips, and my heart melts. How could I go so long without touching her? I must have been out of my fucking mind?

"I told myself I couldn't be with you because of Denver. He's my best friend, and you see the way he is about you and men. But that's not true. That's a convenient lie. He gave me his blessing, and I still didn't move. Then it was my case. It was your parents, maybe. It was timing or setting the scene. None of that was true." I lean forward and kiss her forehead.

"It wasn't?" She looks hurt. I've wasted her precious time.

Shame devours me. "I just didn't think I was good enough for you. *How could I?* I thought, the more time we spent together, you'd figure it out on your own. I didn't want you to realize it two months in when I couldn't live without you anymore."

"Do you feel that now?" She lifts one foot to step away, and my heart breaks finally free from its cage.

I jerk her into my arms. "Are you serious? You're never getting rid of me now." I thread my fingers through her smooth red hair, hold her tight and crash my mouth into her sweet, strawberry lips. I kiss her soft, then hard. Long, then deep. My tongue finds hers, and I ravage every inch until she gasps for air with a tiny moan that nearly makes my cock bust out of my jeans. Months of close calls flash before my eyes. Tortured nights of picturing this perfect mouth on mine come back to haunt me.

I knew once I started, I'd never be able to stop.

"Oscar, you scared me! I thought you changed your mind." She tugs my shirt to pull me close, then slams her breasts against my chest. My busy thumbs flip the straps off her shoulders, and they quickly slide off her arms. She doesn't move to shield her breasts from my view or keep them from my greedy hands. And I can't look away.

The air leaves my lungs---my knees weaken. She's too beautiful for words.

"I want to be gentle, but I don't think I can." My lips, then teeth graze the sensitive flesh of her neck, and she shudders into my arms. My hands cover her breasts, caressing each curve and teasing her pert nipples until she squeezes her thighs and makes the sexiest noise I've ever heard.

"Please tell me if we're moving too fast. We can leave..."

"Leave?" She pulls away and lets the rest of her dress slide off her body. Only a tiny pair of sheer panties remain. "Screw gentle, Oscar. Do you have any idea how badly I need to have sex?"

My heart stops, then promptly restarts. I nod and swallow the lump in my throat. "I have an idea, Darla."

"No, you don't. I bet you've had sex before. I haven't, Oscar.

Do you know I've loved you since I was fifteen years old? That's how long I've waited for you. That's how much I love you." She releases a heavy sigh, covers her breasts with her hands, and turns away.

Darla really waited for me.

Holy shit. I can't believe Little Darla used to love me.

SIXTEEN

DARLA

ONE MINUTE LATER-BROOKLYN

OSCAR'S EXPRESSION HARDENS---IT'S ALMOST UNREADABLE. I shouldn't have mentioned being fifteen. No one wants to see tits and then think those used to be fifteen years old.

It ruins the vibe.

That's why you're still a virgin, dummy. You kill vibes.

I bend one knee and try to reach for my dress. There's no need to make it obvious---like I'm pissed. I just think I've spent too much time topless in the middle of my living room, and it's getting chilly.

"Darla Jones, don't you dare." Oscar pulls his dark blue t-shirt over his broad shoulders and tosses it on the floor. He licks his lips and lets his gaze fall back on my breasts. Or maybe he's looking further south. It's hard to tell when he's so much taller.

I take a small step back to admire his beauty. This isn't the first time I've seen him without a shirt, but the first time I've let myself stare uninterrupted. He's a work of art. My virgin eyes drink him in and revel in every muscle, vein, and oh my word, he's got an erection. My heart trembles with fear or surprise. Maybe both. It isn't tiny. I wouldn't even call it mid-size. That's a lot of cock for a girl my size, but when you fall in love with a big man, you accept the whole man. I can't shy away from my duties.

I clench my thighs and shift my weight, hoping to shield the wet spot forming on these new panties.

He takes one step towards me and unbuckles his belt. "You didn't really wait for me, did you?"

I shake my head and twirl a finger through my hair. "No. I've had many men, Oscar Brennan."

He smiles and takes another step. Then another. His rough hands clutch my waist, slide down my ass and slam me into his chest. It happens so fast, I don't catch on until he wraps my legs around his waist and seals his soft lips to mine. "How many men?"

"Zero." I stare into his steely blue eyes and hold my lips a breath away. "I don't know if I waited for you. But I never forgot you. And I've loved no one else."

"I've tried to behave around you, baby." He squeezes my ass cheeks and walks us towards the stairs.

As we climb the steps, locked in his embrace, I run my hands along the curve of his flexed bicep and tuck my face into the soft flesh of his neck. With one deep breath, I inhale his scent, and the lust simmering inside boils over.

We reach the top and stop at the door to my room. His eyes darken. "What do you want from us, Darla? I know what I want. What do you want?"

His question stuns me. "I want forever. Can you give me forever?"

"That's the only thing I can give you." His lips fall on mine in the sweetest, tantalizing kiss that almost makes me swoon out of his arms. I love this man. And he loves me. Forever.

But I've just about had enough of this shit.

I break away. "Oscar, I meant what I said. Enough teasing."

He kicks the door open with his boot. "You don't know what you've unleashed, Darla. I've been a gentleman for four months.

That Oscar's dead now." He flings me across the room onto my mattress.

I roll around to my knees, slide off my ridiculously wet panties and toss them at his face. "Good riddance, mister. I wanted to kill that Oscar with my bare hands. He's a cruel man."

He holds back his adorable smile and stands at the foot of my bed. His eyes roam my naked body, and he does nothing to hide his appreciation. When his gaze rests on the area between my thighs, he freezes. He's never seen me completely naked.

"Baby..." His voice climbs an octave.

I pose demurely and stare at his jeans. Fortunately, he quickly gets the hint.

With slow sexy moves, his boots come off first. His belt slides off in one swipe. I crawl a few inches closer and lean into a pillow to watch. He unbuckles and unzips, then lets his loose-fitting jeans fall to the floor.

With only his boxers left between us, I do what no self-respecting woman would ever do. I jump to my knees, spread my arms, and hasten him to my side.

"Darla!" He flies into my embrace and tackles me to the mattress. His lips come down hard. His hands are brutal, then soft, squeezing, then caressing but always exploring. Whatever he does, my body stands ready for more, humming like a live wire that sparks to his touch.

"You don't know how much I've wanted to do this." He offers a sinister grin and slides his mouth to my breasts. I wince when his lips seize my nipples---he's not gentle. He engulfs each one like a starving man, winding his tongue around each stiff peak until I curl my body and hold him steady.

His kisses linger on the valley of my breasts, then slip down to my belly. As his shoulders spread my thighs, my wet sex presses against his sculpted chest, and I mark him with my arousal. I thought I'd be embarrassed, but I'm not. I want him to know what he's done to me. He should know I'm ready to be his.

"Darla..." His deep voice vibrates against my skin, and I instinctively jerk my hips.

"What?" I cry out and meet his gaze. His face hovers inches above my pussy.

"I don't think we'll make it to Rye tonight."

OSCAR

SECONDS LATER–BROOKLYN

THIS WAS ALWAYS GOING TO HAPPEN. WE'RE SOUL MATES.

I knew it before I knew it. Do you know what I mean?

I've thought about making love to Darla a thousand times and a hundred different ways, but it always started like this. It always begins with me, face to face, with her unbelievably wet pussy.

I catch sight of her blue eyes, hazy with lust and brimming with curiosity. She doesn't have to watch anything. All I want her to do is feel. I want her to feel my mouth, tongue, teeth, and fingers, and when I'm done, I want her to feel the orgasm that tears her body apart.

But that's only the beginning. Together, we'll feel so much more.

I dip my face, and the scent of her arousal hits me hard. My mouth waters before I've even had a taste.

I breathe her in and take a long, slow lick down the seam of her sex. She bucks her hips, vibrating as she pushes her pussy straight into my mouth. The taste consumes my senses and sparks a primal need I've never felt. This is bigger than us. We'll make something bigger than us.

I spread her thighs wide and lift them over my shoulders. She complies without question. The more I feast, the more quickly she surrenders to my will. With every swipe of my tongue, she hums and calls my name. When my fingers slide inside her, she arches her back and promises to be a good girl. When my mouth finds her hard clit, she sings.

"Oscar!" Her voice breaks. She swallows hard, then tries again. "Please, I need you."

She doesn't need to say it twice. I need her more.

"Darla, I love you." I don't deserve her. I never will. But that doesn't mean I can't spend the rest of my life making myself worthy.

"Oscar, I'm yours." She brings those big eyes to mine. "I'll always be yours."

My heart races with love, and a smile spreads across my face. "I know, baby." She doesn't have to say it, but I love hearing it.

I run my cock through her folds. She's so wet and so fucking ready. I'm dying to thrust in and claim this girl forever, but she's tiny. She saved this virgin pussy just for me, and I need to be gentle.

Just this once. *After tonight, God help her.*

I take a deep breath, hold it and slide in an inch. My body tenses. That's not enough. One more. Darla's grip shocks me.

Goddamn, she's tight. Deep breath. Hold steady, cowboy. Don't hurt her.

Another inch, and I hear a quiet whimper. I don't know what it means, but she makes no move to stop me.

She's so wet, my brain buzzes with adrenaline to push forward and ram this baby home, but I can't. I love her. She's my girl, and you don't hurt your girl.

Darla lifts her tiny hands to my chest and runs them up to my face. Her fingers grasp my jaw until she makes me face her directly.

"I'm not made of glass. Love me, Oscar. You're my man. Love me like my man." She smiles and wraps her legs around my waist.

"I am your man." I take her soft lips in a tender kiss and start slow. I savor every inch and let her get used to my size. Her tight virgin walls tighten their grip the further I go, but the more we kiss, her slick channel sucks me in until, at last, there's nowhere to go.

When I've made my path and broken through, I know she's ready. My mouth crashes to hers. I taste her lips, her breath, and feel her soul in a hot, blistering kiss that seals our fate forever. Darla's mine. Today we make everything right.

I pull out and thrust back in. The pain and friction catch her by surprise.

"Oscar!" She gasps and locks her legs around me. I catch her calves and thrust again.

"Do you want me to stop?" I cup her breasts, holding them for purchase, then thrust again. Her body gyrates beneath me, and I feel myself crumble. I won't last long.

"No!" She lifts her hips to meet mine and takes me in again. "Don't be gentle, Oscar. I need you. Break me and make me yours." Her words trigger a dark animal lust buried deep inside me.

She must read it on my face because she repeats it in a scream. "Break me and make me yours!"

I grip her tapered waist and hold her steady. My fingers stroke her clit with every thrust, building the tension between us and tightening her grip on my cock. When I plunge deeper, her eyes suddenly fly open. She startles, then pants as waves of spasms run through her tiny body.

"Oscar!" She rolls on her side, gasping for air and trembling through bliss.

I curl her into my arms and consider a question I should have asked from the start. I know what I want, but she's twenty-two years old. We have time.

"Are you on the pill, Darla?" Until today, I never realized she was a virgin and never thought to ask.

Our eyes meet and her body slacks. "No. Should we stop? I've got condoms in my luggage downstairs." She sniffles and hides her face. "Just in case things got crazy in Rye."

I tug her back into my chest and hold her as close as two people can be. "I'll grab *my* box from *my* bag. We'll save yours for all the crazy shit you have planned in Rye."

EIGHTEEN

DARLA

THE NEXT DAY- RYE, NY

"Something feels off." We pull into the driveway, and Oscar shifts the car into park. His bicep flexes. My hungry eyes drift to the muscular forearm between us.

I can't turn off my mind.

Last night, all my naughty dreams came true. But today, I need to focus--- we're running on fumes.

Because of my shameless absence from the barbecue I demanded, I set my alarm for 6:00am and dragged Oscar's shell-shocked body out the door by 7:00.

Unfortunately, a night of sexual gymnastics and no dinner brought about a horrible case of the munchies. By the time we reached Larchmont, we couldn't take it anymore. We had to pull over and grab something to eat. Of course, we didn't have to make pigs of ourselves, but these are special times. We're in love.

Oscar pats my lap and offers a reassuring wink. "Relax, baby. I know you feel bad, but we were initially dis-invited. They're lucky you came at all. I'm sure everyone's sleeping late."

I flip the vanity and check my face in the car mirror. "I have great intuition, mister. But you called me baby and gave me a sexy wink. I'll let your lack of faith slide this time." I reach for the car door and get a sassy slap on the opposite hand.

"Let me get your door, please. We won't drive often. You're my girl." While he darts behind the car, I give my hair a quick brush and pop a mint. I'm a real girlfriend now. Oscar's girlfriend. And I have access to his body 24/7. Theoretically, of course. He works. And I have my shoots.

The door swings open, and a sinewy masculine hand reaches out for mine. The touch of Oscar's hand gives me tingles. Shivers of want course through me, kindling a need that won't be denied. I'll suggest a nap before lunch. *Not a real one.* "Hey, baby." I smile, bat my lashes and add a sway to my step.

"You're looking mighty fine, Miss Jones. I don't think I've had a kiss in twenty minutes." He swipes me into his arms, slams me into his hard pecs, and lifts me off the ground. Overcome with sweet memories, I climb him like a tree, crush my lips to his, and dive deep for his tongue.

"Let's find your room." He whispers through kisses, unaware we're not alone.

"Holy crap! You two missed major fireworks!" Andrea ignores we're in the middle of making out and continues to explain. "I can't believe you missed my barbecue!"

When she doesn't depart, we step away from our heated embrace and begin unpacking the car. "Fireworks? They stop the fireworks after Labor Day Weekend." I open the passenger side door, reach for my camera bag and hand it to Oscar. There's no sense in stoking the fire yet. I'll snag him on the way upstairs.

"Not fireworks like firecrackers." She shakes her fists in the air. "It all went down at 5:00am. That's why people are just now getting out of bed." She points to the house, then feels the air for humidity. "Aww shit." She takes a hair tie off her wrist and winds her hair into a topknot.

"Are you going to provide details?" Oscar carries our luggage to the front of the car and double-checks the back seat.

"Yes! Sorry. They canceled the wedding. Your sister and her entourage cleared out early this morning. Your parents and grandparents are still here. Denver and his guests. Harper and I wanted to wait for you guys. Did you know Harper is Angus MacNeil's daughter? Not a love child. He and her mother were married when they were in their twenties. She divorced him for being a big cheat." Andrea bends down to grab a small bag and joins us on the walk to the house.

"Oh, shit." I turn to Oscar. "Did you know?"

He shakes his head and slings the heavier bags over his powerful shoulders. I sigh in admiration and lift my small camera bag to help with the load. He promptly snatches it out of my hands. "No. I knew her old man had money, but she never said who. Why did they cancel the wedding?"

"Demeter found out Angus already split most of the fortune between his three daughters. Even if she outlives him, she'll only get a small amount. Most of his money isn't in his name. And can you believe Harper made me pay for gas on the way here?" She lowers the volume of her voice then looks behind her, checking to make sure Harper isn't there.

I dig inside my purse and retrieve my phone---no missed calls or messages. If I recall, the line of cars by the side of the house looked vaguely familiar. I think the Bugatti belonged to Liam Fitzgerald. "Where's Lana?"

"Asleep with her fiancé. She showed up last night with a big rock and an all-day case of morning sickness. Don't leave until we come up with a plan. I think your Nana wants to throw a party, anyway." She jumps over our row of bags, slides through the foyer, and skitters upstairs like a cartoon roadrunner who's just spotted a coyote.

"What the hell was that?"

Oscar points to a pair of men heading our way. One is my

father and the other man I've never met or seen before in my life. He's almost as tall as my Oscar but broader, more of a beefcake, and a little older. Maybe as old as Liam. He's strikingly handsome with silver-dusted dark hair, crystal blue eyes, and olive skin. I mean, he's no Oscar, but he's kind of hot.

"Darla!" My father approaches and greets us with a warm smile. I'm not sure what I expected, but I'm pleasantly surprised.

"Hi! Daddy!" I lean in and plant a kiss on his cheek. "You know Oscar Brennan."

He offers Oscar his hand and greets him with enthusiasm. My eyes mist. It's a small thing, but I love my father dearly. I want him to approve of the man I love. This doesn't mean much, but it's a start. "Of course, I know Oscar. Good to see you. I'm glad you two could make it. This is my good friend, Judge Dante Fratini, he came up for the wedding, but he's staying for your Nana's disco party."

While Oscar and Dante exchange pleasantries, I stay frozen on the word disco party. The possibilities are endless. Indeed Nana came prepared. What about me?

I tap Oscar's arm and give it a kiss.

He leans into me, smooths the top of my hair, and plants a kiss on my forehead. "I love you, but we're not going back to the city to get disco clothes."

I release a breath and blow it out with an air of disappointment.

"Didn't you say you were going to be a good girl?"

I nod once---I did. And it took little prodding on his part. He played me like a violin.

"I've got a surprise for you tonight. But I need to speak to your Dad, first. Man to man." His eyes flash to mine, and my heart somersaults into my throat.

"My Dad?" Beads of sweat trickle down my hairline. I want to be Oscar's wife. But I don't want my father to hurt his feelings and send him running.

"Do you have a problem with me speaking with your father?" He softens his expression, then smiles. *What a conceited man.* He knows I'm crazy about him. It doesn't matter if my father approves. Either way, we know who we are, and we know what we want. Me and him. Him and me. There's no going back.

"No. I don't. I'll see you when you're done."

NINETEEN

OSCAR

AN HOUR LATER-RYE

ON THE WALK BACK TO OUR ROOM, I TRY TO REMEMBER THE moment I fell in love with Darla. I don't think it was one moment or one day. It was everything.

As small as she is, she's larger than life.

My mom used to say some people fill up so much space in your heart they don't leave room for anyone else. I know what my mother meant. I might feel the same way if I lost Darla, but loving her makes my heart feel bigger. If she wants a big family, and I hope she does, I'll have room in my heart for ten more people.

If she wants it to be the two of us—-that's okay, too.

There's only one Darla Jones, and I won't live without my Darla.

I don't care if people think I'm not worthy. I don't care if they see me as unsuitable.

We belong together. We're a team. *Through thick and thin, until the end.*

As long as she loves me, I rule the world.

"Wake up." I nudge the bed and chuckle into her ear. "You're snoring."

She kicks her legs, flips over, and throws off the blanket. "I do not snore."

"Sorry, sweetheart. You do, and it's freaking adorable." I jump on the bed next to her and catch her hands in mine.

"Baby..." She looks from side to side and wiggles under me. "You kept me up so late. People snore when they're extra tired. And you know... the trees."

I lean forward and kiss her chin, then each cheek, before I settle my lips on hers. Her lashes flicker, highlighting the curious gleam in her eyes. "I spoke to your father."

"What did he say?" She asks with a smile.

"Does it matter?"

She blinks and shakes her head. "No, but I'd like to know. You know I wouldn't let his answer come between us."

"He said he wants you to be happy, and he believes I make you happy."

She smiles to herself but stays silent.

"Darla Juniper Jones, will you be my wife?" The words flow freely, naturally, as if I've practiced them a thousand times.

"Oh, my God! The disco party can double as an engagement party!" She claps and kisses me on the cheek.

"Of course, I'll marry you. You're my man."

* * *

Darla

I DREAMED this day would come. I knew I find something that clicked.

I should have said, someone.

Mrs. Darla Jones-Brennan. Mrs. Oscar Brennan. Mrs. Darla Brennan.

All excellent choices. No need to decide tonight.

Tonight, we dance.

Papa Desmond paid for the lighted dance floor. Nana Junie brought in disco balls, dry ice, and a DJ well known for spinning one hell of a Bee Gees dance mix.

Everyone's having a blast. Harper made up with her Dad, Denver is dancing with the wedding photographer, and Andrea wandered off with the hottest man here---Judge Fratini---the same man she swore she couldn't stand no less than twenty minutes ago.

Despite my sister's cancellation, love is in the air.

Oscar and I aren't the only happy couple celebrating joyous news. Lana and Liam marry in two weeks. Can you believe that? It pays to have priests in the family.

After we met Demeter Tuesday night, Lana went shopping for pregnancy tests. Three positive tests later, Liam popped the question.

It works for them, but I think we'll wait. We're used to waiting. Good things come to those who wait.

In a few years, we'll grow into the happiest family on our block.

What's a few years? Oscar and I have forever.

TWENTY

EPILOGUE-OSCAR
TWO YEARS LATER-BROOKLYN

"Oh, my God, not here." Darla struggles to place her camera away, but I don't wait. I lift her skirt and run my hands down the curve of her ass. Her panties are down before she tucks the lens in its proper case.

"Oscar, it could ruin... oh, Jesus." She pulls the drawstring, then yelps when I slide all the way in.

"You've got this coming, and you know it." I tilt her down, lift her ass high and ram it home. She's so wet, I slide in with ease, ramming through like a careless brute, but her tight walls pay me back. Each thrust shocks me senseless and hastens my release. But I can't come yet. Darla feels too fucking good for a quickie.

"Me? I've got it coming?" She twerks her ass into my hips, feigning innocence while she shows off her moves. "What did I do?"

I slap her ass once, and she holds still, robbing me of her twerk. "Keep going."

She continues, twerking, grinding, swirling her round ass in circles while I watch my cock disappear over and over into her tight little pussy. It's the most glorious sight I've ever seen.

"Where do you want it, baby?"

It's been three weeks since we started trying for a baby. I know they say abstain until mid-month, but I'm convinced that's a myth. Darla's ripe---I can feel it. This week, I've nailed her every day for lunch. No excuses. Today she had a photoshoot, but I ran them off under the guise of an emergency. She shouldn't be working on Sunday, anyway.

Darla wants to be a Mom by her twenty-fifth birthday. And so, help me, God, I'll die trying. I've got three more months to slide it under the wire.

"Where do you think I want it? I want you to shoot that load inside me, Mr. Brennan. I want it deep. Can you give it to me? Can you go deep?" She purrs like a kitten and bends forward, lifting her ass high.

There's no stopping me. My rhythm builds. Tension escalates.

I plunge deeper, thrusting with intent with only one goal in mind---our family. This is what I've always wanted. But Darla had to be ready. And she's ready now.

"Tell me you want it." Her legs tremble as she tumbles closer to ecstasy.

"Yes! I want it. Fill me up, Oscar!" She shrieks, proclaiming it proudly as she tears her blouse over her head and rips off her bra. "And smear whatever's left on my tits."

I gasp out loud. My heart hammers, then skids to a halt. "Darla Brennan, have you lost your mind? We're making our baby."

She shakes her head and thrashes aimlessly as she dives into bliss. "No... I'm... pregnant. Six... weeks."

I slap her ass and growl. "This is why I said you had it coming. Didn't I?"

She screams and falls into my arms, but I keep going, relishing my beautiful Darla, thrusting, pummeling this sweet pussy until I fill her to the brim with so much cum, it douses my balls and gushes onto her thighs.

"Turn over..." I lean forward and press my lips to the nape of her neck. "There's some leftover."

She giggles and falls onto the floor. "You're horrible."

"And you're pregnant?" I slide her onto her back and gaze at her non-existent belly. "How could you keep it from me?"

"You have a birthday coming up. I wanted to surprise you, dummy. Happy Birthday, Oscar. You're going to be a Daddy."

My heart soars. We're having a baby. Darla and me.

I crawl to her side, pull her into my embrace and bask in her warmth. *My Darla's having my baby.*

"You'll be such a wonderful Daddy. I just know it." She sighs and nuzzles her face into my neck.

"How do you know?"

"Because you're the best person I know."

THANK YOU FOR READING!

FOLLOW ME

Matilda is a Texas girl in love with a Philly boy who loves to write dirty books about two people who trip into love and fumble their way into a Filthy, Funny, Happily Ever After.

I live in Austin, with my husband, two crazy Chihuahuas and an even crazier cat. And I spend most of my day writing dirty romance books about older men who fall in love with younger women and make fools of themselves trying to win their hearts.

If you love Dark Romance, you've come to the wrong place. I don't like dark heroes.

I like my hero to be successful, sweet, suave, sophisticated and kind--- and then I want him to lose all his composure and game when he meets the heroine. I want him to turn into a bumbling idiot when he spots the girl of his dreams and revert to a teenage boy in a man's body trying to win her.

I like my heroines to be witty, intelligent, and unshakeable--- who could do just as well without a man—until the hero convinces her otherwise.

I write A LOT OF AGE GAP--because I LOVE AGE GAP ROMANCE. I've got no other excuse for it.

No matter what kind of story it is, my ladies are ADORED, and my endings are always Happily EVER AFTER, not HFN.

To receive a free ebook, join Matilda Martel's newsletter.

Please head to my website to learn what's in the final stages and will be coming out soon!

LOVE REDEEMS

Lucifer walks among us. Leading an army of fallen angels, he still takes orders from above. Good cannot exist without evil. Man's faith must always be tested. It is his job to tempt you. It is your job to walk away.

He hates his role. He hates our world. He hates Man.

But he still seeks redemption.

The Archangel of Light wants to go home and for the first time in 7000 years he has a shot.

Unfortunately, his long-awaited forgiveness will only come if he gives up the only person he's ever loved.

Livia De Lucio comes from the Light. Descended from angels she's caught Lucifer's eye.

Her pure heart intrigues him.

Her beauty enthralls him.

Her love will redeem him.

This is a paranormal, slow burn romance with a devilishly handsome fallen angel, no horns or tail, a woman descended from Nephilim who works for the Vatican, a little bit of violence, archangels, fallen angels, a couple of cardinals, a nun, and a love story about the Angel of Light who finds true redemption in love.

Love Revealed

Yuri Ivanov leads the most powerful Bratva in Brooklyn and commands attention wherever he goes. He's used to making demands and watching people fall in line. Until he meets a young, idealistic assistant district attorney and falls head over heels, obsessively in love.

Rosalind Dunne wants nothing to do with gangsters. Her father was a hitman for the Irish mob and she knows all about the destruction they leave in their wake. Since he died, she's dedicated herself to going after the mob, righting wrongs and saving the world case by case.

Her work is her passion. She has no time for gorgeous, lovesick mobsters with wild green eyes who woo her like she's never been wooed before.

So what if his sexual prowess knocks her socks off. Surely, men this hot are a dime a dozen. Right?

This is the third installment in the Brooklyn Bad Boys Series. Each book is a standalone but they always make more sense when they're read in order.

This book includes, minimal references to an attempted kidnapping and violence. Sexy times. A few peeks at past couples. A swoon-worthy alpha who falls madly in love for his headstrong heroine. No cheating. And a very Happily Ever After.

Love Unleashed

Leo Moretti always gets whatever he wants. No questions. He's his father's son and the blood in his veins is enough to make people fear the consequences of disappointing him.

Except Alia de Alba.

Alia's bold, beautiful and audacious. Her refusal has him on edge. When she turns down his marriage proposal, he incurs her wrath by playing the hero and manipulating her into marriage.

She wants to make him pay, but his hotness makes it hard. He swears they're soul mates but fears she loves someone else.

Can Leo win her heart?

Of course, he can. Leo Moretti always gets whatever he wants

This slow burn turned torrid affair includes one Sassy Latina, one hot Sicilan mafioso, love, lust, sexy times, various Pavarotti references, kidnappings, mobsters, two people who fall madly in love and a guaranteed happily ever after.

Love Interrupted

Igor Ivanov is a mob lawyer who's fallen head over heels in love with a senator's daughter.

Charlotte Wentworth is a Park Avenue princess who's in way over her head.

Madly in love, they defy their families and elope.

But after three blissful days, everything implodes, favors are called in and the two desperate lovers are torn apart.

Powerless and clueless, they part ways and spend four miserable years apart.

When a heartbroken Charlotte is finally allowed to come home, she wants answers. When Igor learns the truth, he wants things made right and more than anything he wants his Charlotte back.

He let her go once, he won't make that mistake again.

Can he convince Charlotte he's the same man she fell in love with? Or will four year of secrets, lies and threats tear them apart again?

This is a steamy second chance romance with two soul mates who fight the odds and crawl their way back home. Grab a cookie, sit into your favorite chair and meet Charlotte and Igor. As always, no cheating and a guaranteed happily ever after!

Filthy Love

Bella Hamilton is on a mission. Her best friend, Ava, is about to marry, and her surprise nuptials have thrown Bella's long-scheduled BFF plans for marriage and babies out of whack.

Never fear, Bella has a plan. She always has a plan. An interview with a young, hot billionaire is the golden opportunity she needs. And since she has no experience with men, she plans to use everything she's learned from years of reading romance novels to lure him into her web.

What on earth could go wrong?

Jude McCormick is nothing like his older brother. He doesn't believe in marriage. He doesn't yearn for a family. He goes from woman to woman and the only thing he longs for is escaping the yoke of his family's legacy.

But then he meets Bella. He's instantly attracted, but she dismisses him. He tries to flirt, but she reacts with disgust. She drives him crazy with lust, but she won't give him the time of day.

At the end of his rope, he's forced to take a harder look and the more he learns about this strange girl, the faster he falls in love.

Dirty, filthy love.

If you've ever wondered what it might be like if your significant other took cues from your favorite book boyfriends—you might like this novella!

Filthy Love is book two of a standalone series. This is an insta-love steamy romantic comedy and as always, this book contains sexy times, a happily ever after and no cheating!

Filthy Rich

Declan McCormick is filthy rich. He's gotten everything he ever wanted, but always wanted the wrong things. At thirty-eight, he's single, works seventy hours a week and comes home to an empty house every night.

Something needs to change.

Ava Jameson has come to New York to finish school. With rich parents, she's gotten everything she ever wanted, except their time. But she swears to do things differently. She has big dreams and one of those dreams is building a better family than her own.

When their paths cross, sparks fly. Declan charges full speed ahead but soon discovers the love of his life isn't so easily impressed and isn't interested in being the heroine of her own billionaire romance.

This is a short, sweet and steamy, insta-love contemporary, older man younger woman, billionaire romance novella with two people who quickly learn the best things in life never have a price tag. Enjoy!

Play Right

Shut Up & Kiss Me

Maestro

Lucky Man

Clever Girl

Magic Man

Agreeably Arranged

There She Goes

The Perfect Nanny

A Hostile Takeover

The Good Girl

The Pastor

The Trophy Wife

My Dad's Best Friend

My Fake Husband

Queen of Two Hearts

Closing Daddy's Deal

The Girl Next Door

And many more!

For updates on new releases click here and a free ebook, click here:
www.matildamartel.com